A CONSCIOUS LIFE

A CONSCIOUS LIFE

Cultivating the Seven Qualities
of
Authentic Adulthood

FRAN COX & LOUIS COX, Ph.D.

Conari Press
Berkeley, CA

For information, contact:
Conari Press
2550 Ninth Street, Suite 101
Berkeley, CA 94710

Printed in the United States of America on recycled paper

Conari Press books are distributed by Publishers Group West

ISBN: 0-943233-76-3

Cover design by Shelley Firth
Cover photo: Freedom, Huang Shang, China 1989
            © Don Hong-Oai
            Courtesy Photos Gallery, San Francisco

Library of Congress Cataloging-in-Publication Data
Cox, Louis, 1940-
    A conscious life: cultivating the seven qualities of authentic adult-
hood / by Louis Cox and Fran Cox.
        p.   cm.
        includes bibliographical references.
        ISBN 0-943233-76-3 (trade paper)
            1. Adulthood—Psychological aspects.   2. Emotional maturity.
    I. Cox, Fran, 1940-   . II. Title.
    BF724.5.C67   1995
        155.6—dc20   95-25519

Printed in the United States of America

10 9 8 7 6 5 4 3 2 1

Love After Love

The time will come
when, with elation,
you will greet yourself arriving
at your own door, in your own mirror,
and each will smile at the other's welcome,

and say, sit here. Eat.
You will love again the stranger who was your self.
Give wine. Give bread. Give back your heart
to itself, to the stranger who has loved you

all your life, whom you ignored
for another, who knows you by heart.
Take down the love letters from the bookshelf,

the photographs, the desperate notes,
peel your own image from the mirror.
Sit. Feast on your life.

Dedication

*This book is dedicated with love
to all our teachers, and especially our children,
Joshua, Sarah, and Laura*

Acknowledgments

We would like to acknowledge the generosity and support of all those who have helped us make this book a reality. We have had many teachers and many fellow travelers on the journey that has culminated in this book. We are grateful for the shared wisdom, love, and friendship along the way.

We would like to single out several people for their contributions. Caroline Whiting proved to be an angel of the muse in getting us started. A special thanks to Mary Jane Ryan, publisher/editor of Conari Press, for her immediate understanding of the message contained in this book and her steady support of it and of us. Thanks to Dr. Thayer Greene for his wisdom, validation, and encouragement. Thanks to our friends in the Creativity Group—Joby Thompson, Anne Macksoud, Richard Mandell, Marilyn Mandell, Geoff Howard, Carole Howard, and Ginny Hamilton—for their love of both the joys and pains of creativity. (An added thanks to Ginny for her computer expertise.) Thanks to Peggy Cosimano and John McCormick for their wise feedback upon reading an early draft. Thanks to Barbara Quick for her skillful editing of the manuscript. And, finally, a heartfelt thanks from Lou to all his clients for their openness to looking within, learning, and creating—all hallmarks of the adult.

CONTENTS

CHAPTER ONE

Authentic Adulthood: The Seven Operating Principles

"The fundamental questions, 'Who am I?' and 'What am I?' arise increasingly in the struggle to find meaning and purpose in life."

—Arthur J. Deikman, M.D.

What is an adult? This is such a fundamental question, and yet neither of us can remember a single time during our youth when someone actually attempted to describe what it means to be an adult. As children, we were often told to "act grown up," but this usually was in reference to suppressing our tears or giggles, accomplishing particular tasks, and in general saving our parents from suffering embarrassment as the result of our behavior. Like most children, we assumed that if we followed the rules of our community, our school, and our family, we would automatically turn into adults at some given point in time, perhaps when we achieved the age of twenty-one. Both of us remember feeling appalled at the idea that one day we would grow up to be like most of the grownups we knew. They didn't seem to be having nearly as much fun as we were when we were very young; and, as we grew older, they seemed to stop growing or learning—which perhaps served as our most vivid intimation during childhood of what it means to be an adult.

Our bodies kept growing, kept maturing. We arrived in our

late twenties with many of the accomplishments judged by our social group to be marks of adulthood—degrees, jobs, marriage, kids, a home, bank account, and so on. But no matter what we did, we had a pervasive underground sense that we hadn't yet become adults, even when we'd left the age of twenty-one far behind. We could find no models of adulthood that personified what we felt like on the inside—like grown-up children who were only pretending to be adults. This sense of counterfeit adulthood erupted into painful awareness under varying circumstances and during different periods of our lives, when we faulted ourselves for any number of "failings"—not being tall enough, spiritual enough, smart enough, sexy enough, for not being savvy enough with our money, for being inadequately involved in the political or social issues of our time, or for just feeling a little bit out of sync with everyone and everything. There always seemed to be a nagging sense that we weren't measuring up, which deprived us of ever feeling completely satisfied with either our accomplishments or our blessings.

As lives on this planet go, we were extraordinarily blessed. It was confusing and intensely embarrassing to live with the dark sense in our souls that something was inherently wrong with us. Like most people, we saw that darkness as the enemy, something to be eliminated or at the very least hidden. This was the skeleton in the closet—after all, we had everything that society says successful adults are supposed to have. As reflective and conscientious people, we did our best to explain it away, work it away, pray it away, "figure it out" away; and then, after these efforts failed, to party it away, sex it away, sleep it away. But the feeling of being an impostor rather than an authentic adult continued to haunt us both.

We believed that we "passed" as adults because we were able

to put together convincing facades made up of acceptable looks, athleticism, brains, and personality. Even though no one else seemed to notice what we thought of as so obviously wrong with us, we never felt like full-fledged members of whatever group we belonged to. We were convinced that "real" adults didn't feel the way we did; we remained vigilant for signs, but no one else ever seemed to express feelings that validated or matched our own. This led to a sense of shame. The best course of action seemed to be to act as if we were adults, even though we didn't feel convinced we were—or at least to act as if we didn't care.

When we reached forty and then fifty and still didn't possess a sense of membership in the adult community, we began to ask ourselves and one another what was really going on here. We had spent years working on both our interior and exterior lives. But we still felt there was so much missing in the answers we had come across to the question: What does it mean to be an adult? And yet we didn't feel any closer to finding the answer. Perhaps, we reasoned, the old priest who had heard innumerable confessions in the course of his forty-five years of service was right on the mark when he answered the novice's question about what he had learned from all those whispered secrets. Without hesitating, the priest replied, "There are no adults."

We are now in our fifties, with three grown children, active professional and personal lives, and a fair amount of life experience behind us. Our perspective has changed, but not without a lot of living and looking within. Over time, we've discovered that we aren't the only people on earth who haven't been able to define or experience adulthood to their complete satisfaction. Although there isn't a lot of conversation about it, many people never feel like adults, no matter how often or how consistently they "act like adults." What has become clear to us is that simply aging and acquiring grownup survival skills doesn't at all guarantee your passage into conscious adulthood.

What Is an Adult, Anyway?

Over time, we've come to disagree with the priest. It's possible to be an adult in our society, but it's a complex proposition involving many basic beliefs and assumptions that may differ from what most people grow up believing and assuming makes an adult. Society's conventional measures of adulthood most often have to do with material success—how much you own, how creative you are with it, and whether or not you get to keep it. Position and status are also crucial to what we're taught to believe in as authentic signs of adulthood: You define your authenticity through your roles as boss, parent, or spouse, or through your success in your chosen field of endeavor.

Useful definitions about what constitutes an adult are rare. Cheryl Merser, in her book *Grownups: A Generation in Search of Adulthood,* notes that in preindustrial Western culture there was no such official stage of life. "You were a man or a woman if you weren't a child, that's all, and the difference for men was one of size, age, and physical capacity; girls became women when they became fertile." In more recent years, sociologists have tended to divide human development into at least three stages: childhood, adolescence, and adulthood. Because both childhood and adolescence are well defined and physically bounded, many people assume that adulthood simply starts when the other two stages have ended.

A newspaper article we ran across recently characterized adults as people who have control. We reeled at the idea. Does this imply that if you control your emotions all the time, you're an adult? Would control of a large company necessarily put you in with the adults? What of the autistic person who controls his emotions all the time, or the corporate head who drinks, womanizes, and ignores his children? Surely *control* is not the operative word.

Another definition of adulthood we've encountered says that an adult is "someone who behaves maturely, responsibly, in a rational manner, with purpose and understanding." We recently heard of a respected lawyer, who certainly meets this definition in her work, who could not make time over a weekend to participate in a conference arranged to help her fifteen-year-old daughter who had just barely survived a drug overdose. Is that the behavior of a responsible adult? Are you an adult if you act responsibly most but not all of the time? What are the cut-off percentages? Does responsibility in your work life count more than responsibility in your personal life? Or is the opposite true? Does a true adult have to like or want all of the responsibilities that go with adulthood?

We know someone who says that an adult is "just a kid with money"; another acquaintance told us that "an adult is someone who knows how to use power, who earns his own way, who knows how to deal with children." It's often implied that raising the question in the first place is symptomatic of *not* having achieved adulthood—if you are an adult, of course you have no reason to ask what an adult is!

For the most part, our society defines adulthood in terms of the behaviors typically associated with adults: Adults do what children and adolescents, by virtue of their dependence and physical, legal, or psychological limitations, are unable to do. According to this definition, there is very little that would separate adults from adolescents. Only legal limitations seem clear-cut. After all, an adolescent can hold a job, start a business venture, even start a family, even if she can't legally drink liquor in restaurants, buy cigarettes, or vote. What we have tried to get at is a more positive definition of adulthood, reached by inclusion rather than exclusion.

But even when we try to define adulthood through positive values, such as honesty and courage, the issues are still far from clear. Honesty and courage in the pursuit of what? Making money? Winning wars? Creating art? Fostering intimate relationships? The very words *honesty* and *courage* have vastly different meanings for different groups of people. Does being honest mean always obeying the law, even if a given law is unjust? Does honesty demand being open to negative feedback about yourself from your friends, employees, and children? Does it mean being truthful even when the truth will hurt someone you love very much? Does courage presuppose the absence of fear? Are there only certain tasks that require courage, such as going to war or speaking out in public; or can simple tasks like getting out of bed in the morning legitimately require courage?

Attempting to define adulthood solely by identifying adult behaviors leads to a misguided emphasis on appearances: It is simply an insufficient way to describe the experience of being a mature adult. There are many grownups out there practicing adult behaviors such as raising families, teaching children, driving cars, balancing checkbooks, and running businesses and governments. These grownups are smart, knowledgeable, talented, successful performers in whatever their chosen work happens to be. But far too often, the learning and changing required to develop their skills in the world of business or day-to-day management haven't taken place in other areas of their lives. Consider the person who is supportive and kind to his coworkers and then goes home and slaps his partner around, or the attorney who couldn't make time for her child, or the father who says "I love you" to his little boy and then leaves him alone with his raging alcoholic mother.

As our perspective changed, we began to see that there are crucial differences between being grown up and being a mature adult. *Adulthood is an internal affair, a state of mind, whereas being a grownup has to do with performing a given set of behaviors.* When we define adulthood by behaviors, we get caught in creating fixed forms. For example, in a large subculture in our country, the ideal model for the adult male is a guy who "uses his head," "keeps his emotions in check," "knows the value of a dollar," believes that "the best man wins," and knows "how to handle women." The real-world embodiment of this set of parameters would be a man who is clearly uncomfortable in the world of thinking, out of touch with his emotions, convinced that his body is merely a vehicle to get around in or an entity to be relieved, limited by the fear of scarcity, unable to genuinely cooperate with others, and manipulative at best in his dealings with the opposite sex.

Such a model is doomed by its inflexibility—and flexibility is a must for psychological health in times of rapid change. There's bound to be trouble when the knight-in-shining-armor tries to swim in the seas of life. Heavy armor may serve you well in particular situations, but in the sea of life it will drag you to the bottom and drown you.

Women are also burdened by outmoded or inappropriate models of adulthood. Old stereotypes abound. A woman is supposed to be beautiful, first of all, so that she can "catch" a man. Any deviation from the model—such as being overweight—is a sign of her failure. A woman needs to know how to use her "feminine wiles" to get what she wants, and yet her needs and wants are supposed to take second place behind those of her parents, husband, and children. Women who challenge their men are "ball busters." A good woman is always there for whatever loved ones need her. A really good woman should be able to have a brilliant career in the outside world as well as fulfill all the traditional roles fulfilled by her mother and grandmothers. She should be a tiger at work but a milk-cow at home. Her children should never lack for any maternal nurturing or attention because of the demands of her career, but her career had better not suffer because of her duties at home. In other words, a tenable model simply doesn't exist.

Grownups Versus Adults

We have come to see the fixed models of maturity that we grew up on as "dress-up" models rather than the genuine article. At best, they're "big brother" and "big sister" models. They took us a certain distance; but, if we're to progress to the next stage in our evolution, these armored old shells must be wriggled out of and left behind. These sets of supposedly adult behaviors are what we are calling the "grownup" (as opposed to the adult).

Being grown up, as it is understood in this country, is not true adulthood, but rather a child's view of adulthood. That's because the models society has created for adulthood have evolved more from people coping with widespread deficits in childhood training and education than they have from the actual experience of adulthood. These models of "adulthood" have serious negative consequences in the physical, personal, social, political, and spiritual life of our culture.

We've articulated a list of twelve core beliefs that seem to underlie most people's ways of approaching a definition of adulthood. If the beliefs sound childish, it's because they are formed in childhood. The problem is that they usually aren't replaced by more rational and authentically adult ways of thinking and feeling, even after childhood has been left behind. Operating out of these beliefs inevitably leads to a sense of disappointment and unhappiness. How many of the following statements strike a chord with you?

1. Your facades (personality, status, income, deeds) represent who you really are.
2. What you plan to have happen must happen exactly as planned if it is to have value.
3. You should be able to produce what you say you want immediately.
4. How you see reality is how it is.
5. When you get what you really want, you'll be satisfied.
6. You don't need to pay attention to your harmful behaviors, even when they keep repeating themselves.
7. Life should be easy because you deserve to be treated well.
8. Nothing can hurt you unless you let it.
9. You don't have to listen to your body.
10. You are in control of your mind.
11. If you behave in the right ways, you will be spared pain.
12. You can grow up to be somebody other than who you are.

If these twelve beliefs represented reality—and many people, consciously or unconsciously, wish they did—you would never have to learn new things as an adult, make mistakes, make reparation, work hard, be creative, get to know your interior world, or really consider others.

There is little understanding in our culture that being an adult is an ongoing process of learning and self-correcting: Life is always changing, revealing what was previously unknown and unplanned for. As Garrison Keillor put it in a column responding to the angry, cynical voter, "In the adult segment of your life, Angry Voter, in the part of your life that comes after your parents kiss you good-bye and kick you out, the future is always uncertain. Even in the past the future was uncertain, and it always will be." We want the future to be nailed down, to come with a written guarantee, but recognizing and moving with its contingency is one of the most important abilities of the adult.

One of the marks of true adulthood is the recognition that what goes on in your interior life manifests itself in your exterior life, whether you like it or not, whether you want it to or not, and whether or not you acknowledge it, or even understand that it is happening. In this society, we take for granted that it makes complete sense to learn about the physical world so that we can travel in it more effectively, more safely, and more pleasurably. Doing so is part of becoming a grownup. But we are still far from taking it for granted that a similar exploration of the interior world of the psyche makes such sense. Many people still believe that noticing and exploring interior experience is self-indulgent, overreactive, elitist, esoteric, unproductive, or even crazy.

This might be exactly why people in our society have no clear sense of adulthood. In his book *Shame*, Gershen Kaufman has this to say about why so few people are well prepared to become conscious adults: "The kind of preparation so many young people have seemingly missed stems from not being able to know how another human being, particularly one older and wiser, actually behaves and lives on the inside."

Learning about the internal world brings many benefits to the person willing to put in the time and effort. The lens through which we perceive and interpret our experience is an internal, subjective one. If this lens is distorted, our perceptions and interpretations will be distorted as well. The ramifications are legion for all aspects of our lives, from the way we treat our bodies to the way we treat our poor, from our failures of judgment in personal relationships to our failures of judgment in responding to political crises around the world.

The Principles of Conscious Adulthood

Your inner world, seen through your own subjective lens, is where you directly experience your beliefs, sense of meaning, values, bonds with others, grief, fear, joy, union, and all manner of strange and wonderful things. It is where discovery and learning and creativity take place. What does it mean to be an adult within this interior realm? What are adult behaviors in this sphere of existence? For example, how do authentic adults respond internally to their emotions, values, spiritual experience, or sense of loss? Would that internal response differ from a child's? Is it here, in this territory, that we can form a clearer and more useful model of adulthood, one that we could actually explain to our children, and model for them through the expression of our own attitudes and behavior?

Our own explorations have led us to answer, *Yes*. We have come to see a new paradigm of adulthood, embodied for us in seven bottom-line operating principles or core beliefs. The adult qualities we want can be drawn from understanding and practicing these seven principles.

1. I am here, and you are over there.

2. I am safe and sound inside my own skin.

3. I am curious about everything that goes on inside me.

4. I learn from my emotions.

5. I know there is nothing but now.

6. I always have power.

7. I always have limits.

We see these internal realities as essential to an individual's experience of conscious, authentic adulthood and the qualities which define it. The seven operating principles have to be discovered internally and recognized as the territory underlying all our behavior. They color behavior, giving it a certain "feel," meaning, and power, but they are not the same thing as behavior. Rather, *they are the ground from which behavior emerges.*

Grownups—acting out of the false beliefs acquired during childhood—can be very skillful at performing adult behaviors without being in possession of an adult state of mind. Their internal experience of their lives will be completely and radically different from that of the person who has internalized the seven principles listed previously.

Realizing these principles creates a state of adulthood inside you—your inner world is filled with opportunities for learning and growing. You feel rooted in the inner safety of knowing that your existence and value have always been beyond question. You understand that the mistakes you make, or the losses you suffer, are not emergencies. Strong emotion is cause for reflection, not shame or panic. Even at those moments when you feel like you're dying inside, you don't run away from your own experience, because you understand that even horrible, painful experiences are opportunities for growth. Your inner muscles are strengthened, and you reaffirm your sense of trust in yourself and your self-love. You know that what counts is being in the here and now. You know that your personal power is inside you and that it's there all the time; it's always available. Finally, you know that you're not omnipotent, and you accept your limitations as well as all the unknowns that are part of the package of being alive.

We don't profess to know the whole story of conscious adulthood. Perhaps, as is the case with evolution, becoming an adult is an ongoing process with infinite possibilities for adaptation and change. There is no definite point of arrival, no plateau when we know we have arrived. There is only the journey.

Explorers in an Uncharted Land

This book catches us in the process of discovering as we go along what it means to be an adult in our time. We can convey to you what we've learned so far—our "bare-bones" paradigm of adulthood. You'll probably find this to be radically different from the ways in which you've heard adulthood described before. Our quest has been undertaken without a map or a model, and this is part of what has made it tricky work. At the junctures when there has been no cultural stamp of validation that says, "Yes, that's it," we've found ourselves wondering: Are we making this up? Is this real? Like explorers in a strange land with unfamiliar flora and fauna, we have frequently turned to each other and asked, "Do you see what I see?" or "What could *that* possibly be?" And yet these very uncertainties are part of the story we're trying to tell. Exploration is *characteristic* of the experience of being an adult. (How different this is from the widely held notion that exploration is the exclusive realm of children or of odd, childlike "dreamers"!)

Throughout this book, we will be referring to the *adult* or *conscious adult* in contrast to the *grownup*. Please don't read any smugness into our use of the terms. Adults, as we define them, are not automatically wise, nor are they exempt from making huge errors of judgment. What adults do have is the simple knowledge that they are situated inside their own skin in a way that gives them the freedom to learn about themselves and the world in an ongoing process of discovery.

This conscious adult self is nascent in everyone. If you were lucky in your development, your adult may be operational a good percentage of the time. In those times and circumstances when the adult is not at the helm, the grownup runs our lives on a kind of automatic pilot. Which entity is steering the boat at any given moment depends a lot on how willing and able we are to be in that moment with full awareness. The more we cultivate the internal stance of adulthood, the more we will inhabit a place of inner security and peace.

The implications of this new paradigm of adulthood for the future of personal relationships, teamwork, communities, social and political interactions, and international relationships are deep and broad. First of all, the adult is absolutely clear that perfection is an illusion, and learning is what it is all about.

This freedom from the tyranny of the need to be right removes all basis for combat and opens the door to inspired, self-interested cooperation. If there is no real emergency in making mistakes, in not knowing, in being vulnerable, in having both power and limits, I can be here with you no matter what. It will always make the most sense to me to work it out with you, rather than try to prove that I'm smarter (more powerful, sexier, and so on), whether you are another individual, a group, or a nation. If you are stuck in being a grownup, I will recognize you as such and still realize that there is no emergency, unless you try to physically harm me; and even then I will be in better shape to deal with you because of my basic trust in myself.

We don't know of one person who arrived in "adulthood" with all these principles in place. Like everything else worthwhile in life, the state of conscious adulthood has to be practiced and learned, requiring both feedback and guidance. What we are offering here is an in-depth examination of each of the seven principles, and suggestions for how to cultivate them.

Before we begin, let's take a closer look at how the grownup gets created. For it is in understanding where at least most of us are starting from that we can each begin to consciously develop the healthy adult within us.

CHAPTER TWO

Childhood's End: The Emergence of the Grownup

"When a child's boundless powerlessness never finds sheltering arms, it well be transformed into harshness and mercilessness."

–Alice Miller

The experience of adulthood is to childhood as the experience of up is to down. The one does not exist without the other; to know one you must know the other. Adulthood makes sense only in that it is different from childhood, both quantitatively and qualitatively. We seem to be clearer about the quantitative differences—grownups are bigger, stronger, know more, have more skills, and so on. The qualitative differences, on the other hand, have been the source of a lot of confusion.

Intellectually, most people would agree that their experience of being an adult is tremendously connected to their experience of being a child. And yet, on a day-to-day basis, those connections are usually forgotten. Most people operate as though their present experience and patterns of behavior had no dynamic or crucial relationship to their childhood. Then they were children; now they are adults. They might admit, "Yes, I'm using some of what I learned in childhood"; but this awareness is usually limited to their intellectual and physical accomplishments, such as having learned to add and subtract or how to walk. The notion that we carry beliefs, attitudes, self-perceptions, a world view, and physical styles based in childhood learning—and that these are actively affecting us at any given moment—is only beginning to dawn in the general consciousness.

With all his limits, Sigmund Freud stuck a compassionate wedge in the door to our understanding of childhood and its impact on our adulthood by recognizing two things:

1. Children have feelings, including deep pain, terror, and shame.

2. Many of those difficult feelings can live on within us, both in their original form and in our defensive, compensatory, grownup efforts to keep them at bay.

In conjunction with these insights, Freud identified an active part of us that isn't conscious but is nonetheless operational all the time. What we've learned in the past colors our every present moment. Time isn't linear for the human psyche, but exists in a kind of fixed time warp, so that experiences from the remote past are always at the ready to affect our adult sensations and capacities.

Not only will the past show up in our current behavior in the most surprising ways, but the felt experience of our childhood is always within us. Freud and those who followed him (see Erikson, 1980; Greenberg & Mitchell, 1983; Maslow, 1971; Miller, 1990; and Seinfeld, 1991) have provided us with tools and techniques capable of shining light on the trove of information in our buried personal histories. Such explorations are not meant to chain us to the past, lamenting what didn't or couldn't happen then, but rather have the potential to help us see the motivations and expectations that affect our present lives.

What is critical is not necessarily how Freud or anyone else might interpret what they saw in the unconscious, but that we have gained awareness of and access to that part of ourselves in a way that allows us to learn from it. Freud directed the Western mind's attention *inward* to the private world of emotional meaning, personal icons, judgments, instincts, and our most deeply held assumptions about the world; to the fact that human consciousness has gradations and layers, from the deeply unconscious through semi-consciousness to fully conscious awareness.

In the evolution of psychological understanding that has followed Freud, we have slowly made our way to a fuller awareness both of the uncanny inner strength of children *and* their incredible inner vulnerability. Grownups cannot appreciate this knowledge so long as the awareness of their own interior world is blocked or significantly limited. Such awareness bears directly on our ability to see and strengthen our true powers and to accept and work with our true limits. The conscious integration of these opposites into our adult understanding of children is crucial to their growth as well as to our own.

Children's True Nature

If we take the time to look, it is relatively easy to identify some universal characteristics of young children. Judgments or evaluations about the worth of these characteristics may vary from culture to culture, but their presence in young children is generally agreed upon (given a healthy physiological system and a minimum of early psychological damage). We would like to review these characteristics briefly. They are the ground from which a conscious adult emerges.

1. Kids Are Curious

Children want to see, smell, taste, touch, hear, feel, move, explore, take apart, put together, look at upside down, and so on—all because they are interested in experiencing, in knowing for its own sake. They seek new and different experiences. Any parent who has been offered a taste of a mayonnaise and sugar sandwich or a pickle and ketchup snack knows what we mean. Kids want to experience and expand the powers that allow a greater range for their curiosity and contact with the world. As Peter Senge, a leading thinker about organizational development, says: "No one has to teach an infant to learn. In fact, no one has to teach infants anything. They are intrinsically inquisitive, masterful learners who learn to walk, speak, and pretty much run their households all on their own."

The direction of this curiosity may vary from child to child, and in any one child over time. Some kids may end up being more curious about an internal process, such as thinking or playing with numbers, whereas another may find an external process—like taking toys apart—to be more interesting. But regardless of the direction of their intellectual leanings, all children love to know, learn, and master.

Being in the constant presence of this relentless curiosity may drive certain people crazy; and it can draw a kid into all sorts of potentially dangerous situations. But so long as a child's spirit is intact, the desire to explore and learn is very powerfully and energetically there.

2. Children Are Intimate

You might say that kids are born into a state of intimacy. All channels of communication are open to infants—other people's touches, sounds, odors, movements, moods, fears, fatigue, dependence, anxiety, and especially their love. An infant is tuned in to its mother or father's very muscle tone and pattern of breathing and gathers tremendous amounts of information from the subtlest nonverbal cues. In other words, young children seem to live in that place visited by adults only at times of extreme closeness with another person. Even the slightest shifts in emotional qualities register very clearly and palpably. When adults are in this state of receptivity, their capacity to know and experience wonder suddenly expands. This state can be experienced in relation to any "other," whether this is a person, a story in a book, an animal, the wind, a mountain, an idea, or whatever.

This open, receptive quality in young children is a source of both power and vulnerability. The power lies in the sense of connection, meaning, and validation that intimacy with another brings. The vulnerability lies in the absence of a barrier to the wounding communications that may be delivered, often unconsciously, by the other person involved. Two of the important developmental tasks faced by children are to learn to determine whether an experience is coming from inside or outside his psychic or physical space, and to develop the capacity to organize all external as well as internal stimuli. Without the completion of these two tasks, the internal and external world would be experienced as overwhelming and chaotic.

3. Kids Are Spontaneous

This quality of uncensored responsiveness is what allows the incredible aliveness of children to shine through. Their love, anger, sadness, joy, confusion, clarity, excitement, boredom, fear, trust, pride, and shame are all quite visible. The idea of hiding or denying what one is experiencing is not a part of the child's natural repertoire; the notion that self-expression can be risky comes only later. A child responds with all of her faculties—her body responds with movement, her voice responds with sounds, her face with expression, her emotions with feeling, her senses with all manner of information, her mind with ideas, her intuition with instinctive knowledge, her creativity with alternatives. Children's spontaneity infuses their playfulness with creative spirit. This natural responsiveness is the foundation of later responsibility.

Playing is a major source of learning and mastery for children. It is also, sadly, an ability that many people have lost by the time they've grown up. Suppression of spontaneity in a child leads to a diminishment in the depth, breadth, and creativity of that individual's ability to be responsive, in both the present and future.

4. Children Are Dependent

The physical dependence of children has always been obvious and understood. If a baby is not fed and sheltered, it will die. Human infants cannot possibly fend for themselves. This is accepted universally as part of the natural order of things.

But children are also dependent psychologically. What a child needs in terms of nurturance for his psyche, sense of self, feelings of worth, and ability to experience and express emotions has been ignored, denied, and debated for centuries, and still is. Because these realities aren't physical, it's easy to be confused about them. What is "the natural order of things" in this internal realm?

Grownups often get uncomfortable when this inner landscape is approached. To acknowledge our dependency at all is a source of discomfort. Admitting that we're dependent on someone or something else for our survival can be terrifying. It entails admitting our vulnerability and recognizing our limitations. There may be something we need that we don't have and can't get by ourselves. We may even feel that we might perish if we don't get it. Acknowledging our vulnerability is, in effect, acknowledging our mortality. As much as we'd like to be, we are not completely self-sufficient. Just have your oxygen supply cut off for a moment, and your dependency on fresh air comes home vividly.

To feel the reality of our dependence, to know it in our hearts and souls, is at best humbling, at worst terrifying. To explore the dependency of children means to explore our own, and to confront our sense of vulnerability. It also means confronting our true strength—but we can't know that accurately without the conscious acceptance of the fact that we *are* vulnerable. We have the same reluctance to face the experience of dependency in our communities—for example, when it shows itself in the face of a homeless person begging on the street; or a pregnant twelve-year-old; or an old person who looks lost, uncared-for, and alone; or the vulnerability of a planet that is increasingly unable to bear the demands of humankind.

Have you ever been in a restaurant with a baby who won't stop crying? It's a sound that absolutely can't be ignored. It stirs people—some to anger, some to distress, some to compassion, others to embarrassment and shame. The level of tension goes up in passengers on a plane when a baby starts crying. For a baby's cry is about a need that is as yet unsatisfied; it's about dependency and vulnerability. That makes us all nervous.

Somewhere deep inside, we know that a baby's crying means fear and/or pain—and we know what that feels like. Most of us have been trained to silence the cry rather than respond to it. But if we are to better understand and respond to our own and our children's dependency, we need to stop silencing the sounds of vulnerability. We need to listen to the message and reclaim its power and meaning.

As you approach this topic of children's dependency, try to be aware of the ways in which it might be disturbing. Most people have a difficult time with the subject. Try to stay engaged as you're reading, even if part of you wants to find an excuse to turn away. Experience any feelings that come up while you're reading. Look at any memories sparked for you. You might even want to write some of these down as you go along.

How We Get Wounded

The sense of ownership, validity, and acceptability of our own experience is not something we're born with. Babies come into the world without the power to unquestionably own their perceptions, validate them as real, and deem them acceptable (or unacceptable). At the beginning, young children are completely reliant on outside validation as they formulate their identity and learn to trust their own version of reality.

Anyone who has taken a six year old to the pool for a swim will have experienced a child's insistent requests to have his or her experience validated. "Watch me jump in!" the child demands. "I jumped! Did you see me jump, Mommy?" the child wants to know, torn between excitement and disbelief. Children need to validate through a grownup's eyes their emerging sense of identity. It is not just the jump that the child needs seen, but also the "I" that jumped. The power of self-validation is acquired only through the development of a stable, separate, and conscious sense of self, which the adults around us help create. Until we have it, we are psychically vulnerable in a very profound way. As is the case with language skills, it's possible to miss the usual time frame within which a sense of self is usually acquired, and to be handicapped for the rest of life as a result.

There is an incipient owner/validator/approver self in every child, just as there is an incipient adult body. But this incipient self is, like the young child's body, undeveloped and completely dependent for its growth on the care and nourishment of adults. This protoindividual—this evolving interior "I"—needs to be seen, recognized, and accepted by an intimate other. Through this recognition and acceptance, children can begin to own, validate, and evaluate their own experiences—that is, their own thoughts, feelings, sensations, and actions.

This is not just a matter of superficial approval. The child needs the intimate presence of an adult, and a "yes" delivered across the channel of that intimacy: "Yes, I see and sense your experience, and yes, it is yours, and yes, it is real, and yes, it is part of being human." If children are deprived of an adequate supply of oxygen, food, water, or warmth, their bodies will be damaged and they will be at risk of death. Likewise, if a child's psychic body is deprived of its nourishment and shelter, it too is damaged and is also at risk of perishing. Children can be forced into a wholesale disowning, doubt, and devaluation of themselves and/or major elements of their experiential equipment—their capacity to feel emotions or sensuous touch, to think, to move gracefully, or to be angry, to name just a few of these tremendously vulnerable resources.

A child's "I" that does not receive enough of this oxygen is left strangled and gasping for breath and may eventually lose consciousness altogether. We believe this metaphor to be descriptive of the child's experience of abandonment. It is the gasping of that incipient self for the breath of life. All the hurt, terror, powerlessness, humiliation, and rage experienced by someone being physically strangled is felt by a child in this psychic strangulation. These are natural responses in both cases.

They are built into the organism as a protection, a warning that something is vitally wrong. The terror and the rage, in particular, are designed to mobilize the young child to communicate its situation through sounds and body movements to its caregivers.

Acknowledged and Unacknowledged Abandonment

There are basically two kinds of wounds we receive as children. One is an abandonment that is then recognized and responded to as such by a caregiver. It's typified in the story of one of our neighbors, who had a second child seven or eight months ago. She was talking with us one day about what a difficult time it had been for her and described how she had been amazed to suddenly see her firstborn, Kathy, as if for the first time in months. She realized then that she had been so overwhelmed by the demands of the new baby's care that she had disconnected emotionally from Kathy. As a result, Kathy had grown unnaturally quiet and withdrawn—when she wasn't making unreasonable demands. As soon as the mother realized what was happening, she got a baby-sitter for the baby and took Kathy out for ice cream and an afternoon at the park. She found a very cozy moment with her child and then told her, "I know I haven't been paying enough attention to you. You didn't do anything wrong, Kathy. I've missed you and I'm sorry." Of course, it was going to take a number of such afternoons in the park together and many intimate moments before these two could build up their bond of trust again.

The second type of wounding is an abandonment that is not recognized or responded to by a caregiver, but is actually blamed on the child. We've seen this done over and over by someone we know, who is in essentially the same situation as Kathy's mom.

This mother never fails to tell her older child what a pain he is, or to upbraid him for not being "good like the baby." This kind of nonresponsiveness doesn't have anything to do with this mother being evil or flawed or even failing to love her child (we're sure she'd be outraged if we suggested any lack of love on her part). Rather, it flows from a lack of connection in the mother to her own feelings and memories of past hurts, which impairs her ability to relate in an intimate way to her child when he is hurting.

It is this second kind of wounding that can create lasting problems for an individual. When an abandonment is recognized and responded to appropriately, the hurt can be healed and integrated as information into the child's experience of the world. There is a loss of innocence, but not of self. But when an abandonment is not responded to adequately by the caregiver, the wound cannot heal. Since the child feels powerless to affect his caregiver, he must resort to internal expressions of self-directed violence and anguish. He may try to protect himself from further pain by psychically disconnecting from the most vulnerable-feeling aspects of his own experience. It's akin to an animal caught in a trap who chews its own foot off in order to survive.

We are using the word *abandonment* to describe any severing of the intimate bond between caregiver and child. This severing can result from any number of events or situations: a death, a parent who is unable to connect to the child (either temporarily or permanently) on an intimate plane, a parent's rage reactions or overprotectiveness, role reversals (children who are forced to be their parents' emotional caretakers), physical and sexual abuse, parental contempt or indifference, or such rigid expectations that a child is prevented from experiencing and expressing important emotions and sensations—anger, sexuality, pride, curiosity, fear, excitement, and so on.

What distinguishes this type of abandonment is that the child's experience of it is neither seen nor responded to by the parent. Breaking the intimate bond between parent and child creates a kind of tear in the child's psyche. If this tear is noticed and compassionately responded to by the parent, the child suffers a hurt that is validated by the parent as real: It can be owned by the child as something that happens in life, as something that matters. Life is not perfect. Mommy and Daddy are not perfect. The tear heals and leaves a scar. The idealization of the parent suffers a blow, but the bond is reestablished, and the child's self is responded to as valid and important.

If the wounding is not responded to compassionately, the experience of the child's self is denied. The message received is that this tear and this self do not matter, are not real. Children then adapt by learning to bury their emotions and reactions. Such children may evolve into grownups who consider exposure of their shortcomings or needs to be dangerous and unseemly, who dismiss their feelings as invalid, mistaken, or meaningless. We would never require our children to ignore the pain and fear produced by an encounter with a hot stove. We would consider those feelings and reactions as appropriate responses to harm and danger. Why, when we ourselves are the source of pain and fear and anger in our children, do we respond as if there were something wrong with those same responses?

We are reminded of a newspaper story we read recently. A two-year-old girl was found silently riding on the subway by herself. She was taken to a shelter, where it was noted with approval that she was not crying or upset, that indeed "she acted like a little adult." It seemed to us that this child, a mere toddler, must have already had a lot of practice dealing with abandonment to be so skillful in shutting down all her signals of distress, even after she was rescued. And the "adults" dealing with her admired her for being so "grown up" as to suppress the emotions that would be completely natural in her situation. It is this kind of denial of a child's reality that relegates people to growing up without achieving full adulthood.

More often than not, we as parents have a terrible block about acknowledging the ways in which we hurt our children. There is a very powerful shaming prohibition against being an inadequate parent, much less a hurtful one. This results in an unconscious demand for perfectionism, manifested in a need for the parent to always appear right or okay, and for the children to do everything in their power not to disturb their parents' happy assessment of themselves.

There is the now almost classic example of the parent at a Little League game who loses it when his child makes a mistake. When parents find the experience of their own shame to be intolerable, they are similarly incapable of tolerating the mistakes, shortcomings, or weaknesses of their child, especially when these become manifest in a public situation. On top of this, it becomes necessary for the parent's own self-esteem not to see the hurt he has caused his child through his critical attack or attitude. Thus such hurts are trivialized by the parent, rationalized as necessary, and, more often than not, blamed on the child. If these denied abandonments happen consistently enough, the very existence of that child is invalidated. This is manifested in a disowned, discredited, and dislodged sense of self and a deeply internalized sense of danger.

The depth and severity of these unhealed wounds depends on many factors. For example, if the intimate bond is permanently broken at birth or very soon thereafter, the child's self never gets a chance to plant roots and grow, and can remain fragmentary for life. People who suffer these early deprivations in the nourishment of self will have some ways of being in the world that are different from those of people who suffer deprivations later in their development, when they have a better grip on who they are. Recognition and healing are slower to come; change and pain are harder to deal with.

Operating Principles of the Grownup

What we are calling the *grownup* is the amalgam of beliefs, attitudes, judgments, defenses, and feelings that accumulate in any given individual over the course of his or her life. Each of these qualities was initially acquired because it worked on some level during childhood as protection, camouflage, a bargaining chip, or a manipulative tactic. The resulting grownup (really a grown-up child) is the product of unhealed childhood wounds and the internal coping skills developed in response to those wounds, as well as the physical and mental skills the individual has picked up along the way.

The grownup is not a natural internal state, but rather the result of the violation of the natural needs of children. We are not trying to lay blame in pointing this out. The word *grownup* isn't used as a judgment. It's merely a descriptive term meant to stand for people who have not been given the specific nourishment that allows for the evolution of an *adult* (as we're using the term). Such people—and this would include *most* people in our culture—cannot be expected to provide that nourishment for their own children. The natural spirit of a child is actually quite hard to kill. But when you look at the aliveness of young children, and at what most of us settle for in adulthood, it's plain to see that this killing is accomplished almost routinely.

For children in an ideal world, the effort involved in growing up would emerge from the desire for continuous self-discovery. It would entail the development of personal freedom and responsible citizenship, driven by the individual's excitement and sense of personal gratification in being the agent of growth and change.

Being a grownup, as opposed to an adult, means becoming more and more skillful at compensating for and covering our wounds. The goal is to achieve complete invisibility for these wounds (this goal is at the root of perfectionism). In pursuing this goal, the grownup develops a set of internal operating principles, learned in childhood, to survive by. These operating principles are the "bones" of the future grownup, both in the sense that they form the skeleton that props us up, and that they are as intrinsic to our being as our bones are. They are diametrically opposed to the operating principles of the adult.

Here are the seven operating principles of the grownup:

1. I Must Control, Dismiss, or Merge with You

The experience of abandonment is an emergency for a child. It is not a minor hurt or simply a discomfort, but calls forth instinctive emergency responses of terror and/or rage. Abandonment demands resolution. If these emergencies are not treated by parents as significant, the terror and rage intensify. Ultimately, these feelings become too intense for the child to support them. At a certain point, for the protection of the individual's fragile psyche, they are pushed out of consciousness.

These emergency states are kept unconscious in a number of ways. Some children cope by cultivating self-hatred and self-criticism, activated by cues from Mommy or Daddy or other "needed ones" as to what pleases and displeases. Such children become hyperalert in their bid to avoid the pain of future abandonments. These are the individuals who grow up to be "people pleasers." Conversely, some children cope by convincing themselves that they're completely self-sufficient—they don't have any need of the "needed ones." Such children tend to grow up to be rebels or loners, but they're motivated by the same desperate bid to avoid pain. Other children cope by internally merging with their fantasized ideal caretaker, celebrating this person's virtues to the exclusion of all others. In later life these children may grow up to be "love addicts" who become obsessed with one impossible relationship after another. They're also more likely than others to idealize a leader, an organization, a belief system, or a lifestyle with disproportionate single-mindedness and passion. Most of us have experienced some mixture of these coping mechanisms in our own lives.

In none of these three cases can true independence evolve, because a truly separate sense of self is never developed. The grownup is locked into a dance with others based on a denied but exacerbated dependence. As a grownup, I must control your perception of me so that you will continue to be available to me; or I must obliterate your importance to me; or I must merge with you in order to have a secure sense of self. By myself, I am not enough.

2. Appearing Vulnerable or Flawed Must Always Be Avoided

Shame is one response of the child self to being treated as if she neither existed nor mattered, or as if there were something wrong with her. Shame comprehends the terror of being annihilated, intense self-loathing (rage at self), a sense of utter aloneness and isolation, and a terrible feeling of desolation. The inner states of despair and shame are life-threatening in terms of a child's psyche, calling forth a survival strategy calculated to eliminate the feelings and make sure they don't reappear. The only way open to the child is to remove the traits that her caretakers find offensive, and/or deny within herself that she has any need for their approval (in other words, to deny her vulnerability). If I'm smart enough, or good enough, or tough enough, or obedient enough, or don't ask for anything, or do whatever my parents value, I won't have to feel this overwhelming pain. Grownups who evolve from this type of situation have trained themselves to deny their dependency and/or hide their flaws at all cost.

3. I Pay Attention Only to "Reality"

Curiosity in the grownup self must be narrowly focused if not eliminated altogether. There was an expression used by a lot of grownups when we were children: "Curiosity killed the cat." Too many of us have assimilated the lesson that curiosity for its own sake is a risky business. And yet when children are allowed to follow their natural tendency to be universally curious, the results belie the wisdom of that lesson. They learn on their own that they need to keep their eyes open for risks and dangers as they follow curiosity's lead. But when they are shamed for asking a question, curiosity itself becomes a source of pain.

When free-spirited inquisitiveness, exploration, fantasy, and speculation are responded to as bothersome, annoying, threatening, or just plain bad by parents and teachers, a child's natural curiosity gets squeezed into a narrow channel of expression focused almost entirely on the question: How do I survive and navigate this situation in which the expression of curiosity only adds to my danger and potential for experiencing more pain? Children adapt by narrowing the scope of their curiosity to those areas in which it is rewarded by the grownups in charge. They suppress their pleasure in being curious (because if it pleases me, it might get out of hand), and look for the external rewards of approval for compliance and acceptable achievement.

This shifts the locus of motivation for learning from the inside to the outside. Instead of the pleasure and satisfaction derived from the process of learning and mastering something, external rewards become the driving motives—social acceptance, money, control, dominance, or even avoidance of criticism. The joylessness of many classrooms and work environments attests to the squelching of curiosity. Grownups who have assimilated the lesson of curiosity and the cat are cheated of countless opportunities to grow and expand—intellectually, emotionally, and creatively.

4. I Must Control My Emotions at All Times

Very often parents are unresponsive to the child's reaction to abandonment because feelings of rage or terror are intolerable to them. Such parents have the need to immediately quell such manifestations in their child, either through punishment or superficial placating. The child's feelings become the target, as if they were the problem, rather than being responded to as a message about the child's experience. As a result, the parent produces more abandoning behavior and moves farther from intimate contact with the child. The child eventually gets the message that the feelings are the problem, and will begin the internal, lifelong process of suppressing and repressing them. A manner of gut awareness develops: If I don't show or have these feelings (flaws), then at least Mommy will not be so far away, or so angry, or so violent.

There may likewise be feelings a parent requires in his or her child before bestowing approval. The child copes in various ways:

Mommy can't stand my anger, but she likes me to be afraid of her . . . Daddy gets violently angry when I show that I know how pretty I am, but seems to like it when I act shy and demure . . . Mom hates it when I let people see how much more self-possessed I am than she is, but she acts pleased when I show that I'm better than other kids at something. Grownups hatched under these conditions may turn out to be completely unemotional, or allow themselves to be emotional only in certain safe and approved ways. Foremost in importance is never allowing their emotions to be out of control (never allowing the intolerable pain to return).

5. I Must Manage the Moment and Not Let It Surprise Me

When the intimate bond between parent and child is repeatedly broken and the resulting wounds go unacknowledged, a shift is made from a basic sense of safety to a basic sense of danger. Intimacy between parent and child becomes just part of the potential for further pain. If children stay in that intimate space when it's no longer a harbor of safety, they are in continuous danger of reexperiencing the intolerable emotions of abandonment. Not surprising, they tend to flee from further closeness.

The unpredictable aspect of living fully in the present moment becomes terrifying. Children who are wounded in this way will do almost anything to give themselves the illusion of some control, even if it means cutting themselves off from their own moment-by-moment experience of the world. They're effectively cheated of their natural right to savor and explore or be intimate with their own present at any given moment. The past and the future tend to enter their consciousness only in terms of warding off repetitions of the pain.

Such children are often left with no choice but to "grow up

and stop being a baby." This involves shutting down their emotions and focusing their attention primarily on reality—that is, on the outside world as defined by others. The child's intimacy with its own inner world of information is interrupted, and a wall is built around it. This is not the healthy process of separation and individuation that occurs naturally in a child's growth into adulthood; it is a denial of dependence rather than the growth of independence, a forced separation from the child's own alive moment. There can be no surprises, no self-absorption, no letting go, no intimacy, no real rest. All energy goes into the attempt to avoid further pain. Life gets reduced to a series of managed moments.

6. I Have Power Only When I Control, Dominate, or Win

When natural curiosity and intimacy are diminished or eliminated, the sense of one's power and limits becomes distorted. For children to learn what is in their control and what is not, their trust in their perceptions and intuition must be validated. If there is pain or fear or anger, those sources of information must be treated as valid—because they are. The child's internal experience is telling him something that he needs to know about himself and the world. If these emotions are not treated as real, or if they are treated as bad or dangerous, the child is likely to distrust his own senses and be left at the mercy of others to determine what is real and what is not, what is meaningful and what is not. He may be taught or trained, but he will not learn; he will not know through his own self-discovery.

When the permission for spontaneity is reduced or eliminated, and the focus of my attention becomes fixed on the reactions to my actions, I am forced to value my power based on your reaction to it. For example, if using my muscles to move something from here to there is all about gaining your approval (or challenging your disapproval), then the value of my action is completely captured in its effect on you. The experience of my muscles lifting, the carrying, walking, putting down, and letting go somehow doesn't enter into the equation. The exercise of that set of physical powers or skills brings no pleasure or credit in itself.

Many highly successful, powerful people look back on their accomplishments with a sense of disbelief and unreality. They will often say that it "feels like it never happened," or that they have no idea how they got here, how they did it. It often "feels like a fluke," or they feel like impostors. Grownups (as opposed to adults) are deprived of intimate contact with the free, moment-to-moment exercise of their personal powers, the ownership of those powers, and the results they produce. This is so because their power is never discovered as emanating from within.

7. My Limits Are Either My Fault, Your Fault, or God's Fault

For the grownup, limits are seen as embarrassments and faults. To not know something in a work situation is too often seen as something to hide rather than as an acceptable momentary limit and an invitation to exercise a personal power—for example, as an opportunity to learn. Blaming becomes the skill to develop instead of learning, problem solving, creating, and healing. If the grownup learns, he learns late or on the sly. Risks are to be avoided because of the potential for making mistakes. On those occasions when mistakes are made, the grownup either blames someone else or excoriates himself. Wonder and awe are never experienced, since they require contact with our limits and what is unknown or unknowable.

When we can accept that our identity is inviolable, there is no problem recognizing and accepting whatever we cannot do in a given moment. The limit is no reflection on our value: It's part of our momentary experience rather than something universal or eternal. Knowing that we are ignorant or powerless over something, or discovering how little we know, becomes not an occasion for shame but rather a source of humility, awe, and the recognition of both the small unknowns and the Great Unknown that are part of being human.

The Dance of the Grownup and the Adult

Grownups view each day as time to maintain and build evidence that they really *do* exist and *are* acceptable. These are not givens as they are for the adult. If the evidence is coming in, the chronic, unconscious emergency state is muffled, and a high may even be produced momentarily. But there is no bank account built up, even though the funds may be earned over and over again, because the grownup at her core feels worthless.

The underlying objective of all the grownup operating principles is to hide our worthlessness, especially from ourselves. There is no true rest—there are only periods of relief or highs, followed by emptiness that must immediately be warded off by more evidence gathering. The evidence can take all sorts of forms—being good, making money, being all-providing, being needy, being famous, being a rebel, being part of a special group, blending into the crowd, being skinny, being busy, being a victim, being a bully, being a mess, being sexually active, abstaining from sex, and on and on.

Many of us function pretty well as grownups, at least for a period of time. But when the difficulties of life hit hard, the carefully constructed grownup identity can unravel. It is then that feelings of intense fear, powerlessness, and worthlessness—

usually quarantined in a closed-off part of yourself—begin to spread. Often these feelings become manifest when you are forced to realize that you are not in control—for example, in the event of an illness, a death in the family, an accident, a rejection, or a failure.

For most of us, it has taken some kind of painful wake-up call to begin to see our grownup selves as largely a conglomeration of compensatory behaviors, and not our true self. The mother and father who have to deal with the death of their child, the older executive fired suddenly without warning or explanation, the Generation X'er who tries to commit suicide—all come to confront the unhealed wounds in themselves that lie beneath the grownup facade.

The difficult feelings caused by unhealed wounds are present within everyone continuously, but their intensity is usually muted, and the individual's awareness of them may be submerged. The methods for keeping these painful feelings at bay can take many forms: perfectionism, idolatry, prejudice, or blame, to name but a few. When people function primarily according to the principles of the grownup, the major part of their energy is driven by an intense need to avoid consciously experiencing the intolerable feelings locked within their unhealed wounds. It's like having a ball of radioactive energy more or less successfully contained within a lead chamber inside you. Some people's chambers leak enough so that you can see the feelings of fear and worthlessness they carry within them. With others, the chamber is sealed very tightly, and you see only the walls (for example, the need to present a perfect appearance at all times, always having the answer, rigid moralism, and so on).

The problem with this state of affairs is that nothing is done for its own sake, but rather to hide who you really are and to compensate for the feeling of essential worthlessness: to cover your tracks and prepare for the disaster of future exposure. It's as if that radioactive ball has managed to burn a hole in your stomach, and all your experience of self becomes as useless to your maintenance as fast food. You're deprived of any nourishment that sticks to the ribs.

The longing, which is often unconscious, for real nourishment of our sense of self—for "soul food"—is ongoing. When this longing is twisted in our early years, we become confused about both the need and how to fill it. Position, power, money, status, the right partner, or the right set of ideas are the "junk food" substituted for intimacy, connection, self-love, revelation, and acceptance. The attraction to junk food of this kind can lead whole organizations, not just individuals, down self-destructive paths (witness the Third Reich or the debacle at Jonestown).

On the other hand, the principles of conscious adulthood, once contacted, can both heal the hole and provide the "ribs" that nourishment can stick to. When we operate from these seven principles, there's a tremendous sense of relief, of being home, of resting inside our own skin; a freedom of movement in our bodies, minds, and souls; a certainty that we are, and we are just fine, whether we're happy or sad, succeeding or failing, loving or hating—whatever.

Being fully present in the state of adulthood is a blessing. We bless others; we can bless ourselves, in particular those parts of our self that have been painfully distorted or scarred. When consciously cultivated, the operating principles of adulthood form a kind of container—one that holds us without limiting us, that is both infinitely flexible and profoundly strong.

It's important to keep in mind that both these states—the adult state and the grown-up child state—coexist in everybody to one degree or another. Most of the time, the balance between the two shifts from moment to moment.

When the grownup has the upper hand—but, like the Wizard of Oz, is still hiding behind the curtain—the new adult can very gently and firmly enter this inner sanctum and engage the grownup in a conscious dialogue. The trick is to remind our grownup self that the principles we've been operating from are outdated and useless right now. The adult can metaphorically embrace the wounded child within the grownup and say something like this:

I know you're there. I know you're terrified of being seen. I know you may fight me for possession of our awareness. I am not afraid of who you are. I know that the hatred of yourself that you carry has been taught to you. There is nothing about you to hate, to feel shame about. I know you may not believe me or trust me. But I will not go away. I want you to discover that you are safe with me, that I will protect you, that I will listen to you very carefully . . . even though you may not like it to begin with, because you believe that your life depends on not being seen, or heard, or felt, or recognized.

In this way, your adult self can accomplish several things at the same time. You accept the "negative unconscious," including everything known and unknown that it may contain. You apply healing awareness to the unhealed wounds of your inner child. You dramatically deepen your self-awareness by acknowledging the destructive shadow side of your personality. You break the time warp in which your grownup self has been locked by bringing it back into the conscious moment. You gain access to the creative unconscious and the Great Unknown by being fearless in the face of the need to hide your internal world from yourself and others.

The process of moving between the grownup and the adult is about embracing not only the light and the darkness in our lives, but all the gray areas in between. This is not necessarily an easy task. It's been our experience that as soon as we put in place a new piece of internal adult identity, the grownup guards in charge of maintaining the old order begin their loud destructive clamor, tossing around weapons like doubt, fear, weariness, confusion, depression, and shame. Real change always includes a confrontation with these guards. Throughout this book, we'll identify their methods and means of disruption, and shine some light on their tactics, which so often include guilt and blame.

The human race is collectively engaged in the process of waking up to who and what we are, both as children and as adults. Building on this evolution, we hope to move you toward a clearer understanding of what it is to be an adult human being at this time in the history of our world.

CHAPTER THREE

I Am Here, and You Are Over There

> *I exist as I am, that is enough.*
> *If no other in the world be aware I sit content,*
> *And if each and all be aware I sit content.*
> *One world is aware, and by far the largest to me,*
> *and that is myself.*
>
> —*Walt Whitman, from* Leaves of Grass

I am here, and you are over there. The simple but profound awareness that we are separate beings—not only in the outside physical realm, but also in the internal psychological realm, the realm of the self—is the first operating principle of adulthood. It's the only ground in which all the other principles of adulthood will flourish. Grownups cannot hope to become adults until they've assimilated this first basic truth about their independent existence in the world.

Many people live with a deep personal doubt about themselves, often without being able to put it into words (or even being fully aware of it). They may doubt their essential value or right to exist. They may question their ability to survive in the world, not just as a physical being, but as an individual with an internally stable and valuable identity. They live without the certainty that their selfhood is a given that cannot be threatened or compromised by anyone else or by any set of circumstances short of death.

Such doubts are kept at bay by a variety of "grownup" strategies that work until you are rocked by changes in your financial, personal, or professional situation. With one horrible blow to your ego, with one slip in your careful portrayal of who you are, with one tragedy that cuts to the heart, your sense of your own value can plummet like suddenly worthless stock. You may fall to the point where you question your very reality and right to exist.

Identity and Belonging

We want to explore the adult phenomenon of psychological separateness, by which we mean a conscious awareness of an indestructible and discrete psychological identity. This awareness begins with the knowledge that you are physically separate from others.

Your personal awareness and experience of the world emanate from inside your own body. That's the bottom line. Another person's thoughts, feelings, beliefs, and attitudes about you can't touch who you really are. You are here; they are "over there." This may not always feel true to you, but it is; and until you internalize the truth of it on a gut level, you won't feel safe in the world.

Far too often, we don't act from the truth that our psychological reality—our most personal inner reality—is contained within the skin of our bodies. This inner, psychological space is as real, valid, and inviolate as the territory you occupy inside your physical body. Just as your heart is your heart, and your lungs are your lungs, your essential selfhood and identity are yours and yours alone. No one can change them by talking to you or hurting you or even by loving you. Your selfhood and identity are safe, and their integrity will be intact as long as you're alive.

Knowing this fact intellectually and living it are two entirely different experiences. For instance, a child's thoughts about his mother are not the same thing as the reality of his mother. As connected to her as he may feel, her reality is separate from his thoughts, feelings, or physical sensations. Infants and young children are unable to make this distinction until their perceptual and intellectual abilities mature to a certain degree. Learning to discriminate between oneself and others is an incremental and essential part of the process of growing up. When this process doesn't unfold successfully, a grownup results rather than an adult.

In his 1991 book, *Trances People Live,* Stephen Wolinski suggests that a prevalent "trance," or misconception, is the belief that everybody is in the same reality. Only when people wake up to the fact that their individual reality is not the only one can they understand the meaning of *I am here, and you are over there.* Such an understanding is the beginning of true membership in the human community, and an entrée into living in the moment.

Many years ago, a teacher of Lou's told of witnessing a seven-year-old boy coming into a deepened awareness of *I am, and I am separate.* The boy had been getting more and more frustrated with his father during the course of trying to explain something to him. The father was very interested, but was having trouble grasping his son's thoughts. The boy asked him in exasperation, "Why do I have to keep explaining?" The father said, "Well, I'm not you. I'm not in your brain: I can't see what or how you are thinking in there. You are the only one in there. If I'm going to understand, you have to explain it to me." The boy looked a little surprised, then kind of sad and pensive; and then, all of a sudden, he beamed. He started dancing and shouting, "I am me!" and went running off with a thrilled look on his face.

One result of this internal awareness of a separate "I am" is the sense of security it produces along with a sense of one's place on the planet. The feelings, if translated into a monologue, might sound something like this:

I belong here, I am already home. It's no longer a matter of somebody else deciding whether I deserve a place here, or whether I'm worthy of belonging among other people. I exist, therefore I belong. It's a given that I have a part to play in the human drama. This isn't something I have to prove. It's not a matter of fitting into somebody else's conception of who belongs and who doesn't. It's not a matter of being good enough or worthy enough. I know that I belong, as does every other person here on this planet, both individually and in relationship to other people, the animals, the plants, the sea, the air, the earth. This knowledge gives me a sense of security as I move among other people. Regardless of what they think of me—whether or not they want to include me as a member of their particular club—I know I belong on the earth and among the human race, and I can take the responsibilities and rights inherent in belonging.

Within a given group of people, I may find myself playing the role of the outcast—they may not want me to be a member of their club. Perhaps they help define themselves by judging and rejecting me. If that's the case, that's their problem, not mine. Adults don't need to define themselves in relative terms. They are who they are. I don't have to prove the value of my existence by pleasing or displeasing people, proving that I'm the same or different, better or worse than anyone else. Adults don't have to prove anything about their worth and merit, because they know their inherent value. This, in turn, places them in direct contact with the value inherent in everyone and everything else in the world.

For the adult, there is no effort toward selfhood, no straining for validation from the world. You don't have to twist your identity to fix it up or trick it out or tone it down. None of that—who you are at your core is a simple given.

Try to get a sense of what it would feel like to know this, even if it's something you've never experienced before (and most people never do). Let yourself entertain the possibility. Sense the ease and security and inner safety that would envelop you as you move either in your own private world or in public. Such knowledge is a treasure far more valuable than the usual treasures people long for—money, fame, fortune, glamour, romance. In fact, what it gives is at the heart of what people hope to gain from those things: a sense of worth and validation.

The concept is so simple and yet it's something that few people have internalized. Once you do know, there's a kind of ease about it, a comfort zone in which you're free from the state of chronic emergency that constantly nips at the heels of the grownup's psyche.

Being and Value

Adults are secure in their knowledge of their own boundaries. These go beyond the obvious physical ones to the internal boundaries of a separate and intact psychic identity.

Grownups are people who have not had the experiences to help them understand that their identity and selfhood are as durable as the earth beneath their feet. They operate under the illusion that the supply of "oxygen" needed to keep their psyche alive and well is under someone else's control rather than their own. They feel a life-and-death dependence on other people based on this fallacy. Like Dorothy before she was told the secret of the ruby slippers, people spend their lives on futile quests for lifesaving help from others, when all along it's completely in their own power to get what they want and need.

A heart-and-soul understanding that we exist as separate, interior beings allows us the direct experience of our inherent value and the basic integrity of our selfhood. Because grownups are trained to ignore and devalue their internal world, they're deprived of this solid ground of knowledge. In contrast, the adult has either grown up in circumstances that encouraged this internal sense of a separate self, or else has made an effort to create it later in life. In either case, the adult feels safe and solid whereas the grownup can never feel completely secure.

Because of the way we are brought up, people often have the whole thing backward. They harbor the belief: I have value, therefore I exist . . . If I do this for people, or do that for people, or make this kind of contribution, or behave this way, or look that way, or have this or have that, then I exist, then I am, then I can finally feel safe and secure in my being.

Once you really are in contact with "I am here" in a genuine, internally experienced way, you automatically contact "I have value"—and nobody can do anything about that, no one can alter it. The experience of internal value is *inherent* in the experience of being.

Again, the adult's feelings might translate into something like this:

I'm here and nobody can change that. They can think anything they want. They can believe anything they want. It doesn't touch the reality of my interior existence. It may alter my exterior circumstances, but I can deal with that, even if it's difficult. This I, this me, this person is here. Just in this simple knowledge, I come in contact with my value.

If, like most people, you weren't raised to have a strong sense of your own inherent value in the world, you'll have to start assuming the stance of the adult, even before you've really contacted internal adult realities. You have to start somewhere. It will take some time experimenting with the feelings before they open a path to your real nature. But when you internalize the basic sense of "I am here," the rest will follow naturally—the particulars of your value, how you contribute in an individual way, the gifts you have, the contributions you make, the things, skills, or experiences you acquire. Once you know your basic value, all these particulars become an expression of that value. They're not proof of it— because your value is a given that doesn't need proving. They're an expression of your value. Once again, knowing your internal value automatically allows you to know the value inherent in others.

Personal value for the grownup always lies in accomplishment and possessions, only in doing and having, not in being. Being is an internal experience. If, as a grownup, I have been trained to ignore my inner experience, I will have difficulty connecting with the experience of being. It probably won't make any sense to me at all. Being is an internal state, not a thought or an action or a physical event. Knowledge of this state is dependent on being in it, on "touching" it internally. Many people have not had this experience (or, more accurately, have lost contact with it); so the whole concept sounds like nonsense or "psycho-babble" to them, depending on their prejudices.

—
55

Mastering the Tool of Internal Consciousness

In this transitional stage of our evolution, all of us have been raised to be grownups, not adults. Adults on this planet are like the primitive humans who discovered they could use fire for their benefit. They were still the same primitive humans they were before the discovery, but now they had a tool that would deeply affect the course of their evolution. There were probably humans who feared fire during its transition from an unpredictable force of nature to a useful tool. Those primitive humans probably thought the ones "playing with fire" to be the primitive equivalent of "crazy," or maybe they saw them as gods or demons.

The equivalent to the tool of fire in this phase of our evolution is the tool of internal consciousness—that is, consciousness or awareness applied to the inner experience of selfhood. This tool has consequences for our experience of emotion, our internal attitudes and belief systems, our imagination, intuitions, and thought processes. It will help us approach our ways of knowing, learning, and self-awareness with as much curiosity and deep interest as we have in former times applied to our awareness of the physical structure of the world, or the work we do, or which team wins the World Series, or which movie wins the Oscar.

As we gain knowledge of the outer world, we also come to appreciate how much we don't know or understand. The situation is the same as we gain knowledge of the structure and content of our internal world of selfhood. We come to appreciate how much there is that we don't know. We begin to see that there are powerful forces acting within us on an unconscious level. These forces may be completely hidden from view until something approximating an internal microscope brings them into focus. In fact, the understanding that "what I am aware of about my internal self is only a very small portion of who I am" seems to be just over the borderline that separates being grownup from being adult.

In a paradoxical fashion, adults recognize their lack of awareness about much of the content of their inner lives, whereas grownups are unaware of any hidden dimensions to their selfhood. The adult knows there is "something in there." The grownup, at best, says, "If there is something in there, it's not worth knowing about." The adult knows he's got a grownup inside him operating by a set of principles antithetical to his—in other words, that he is divided internally into an adult interested in expanding his internal awareness, and a grownup interested in maintaining his unawareness and minimizing any discoveries that might cause him pain.

We're interested in describing and fostering the evolution of awareness that finds its ground in the reality of "I am." For the purposes of this book, we focus on this "I am" as being located in the body. We do not deny the possibility of out-of-body experiences, but will limit our description to the value of being grounded in "I am" within one's own particular body.

Eventually, such awareness can produce a sense that you *fill* your body, rather than just *have* one. Your awareness extends into every part of your body and courses through it. You are present in your body, and, as a result, your body feels comfortable, relaxed, easy, trustworthy, known, and appreciated. The way it moves, the way it feels, the things it can do, the actions taken with it—all are experienced by you consciously and appreciatively. No special effort is involved. This kind of awareness is second nature to the adult.

Most people have experienced moments of this kind of awareness, when they felt relaxed and particularly at ease, or graceful in some way, or "out of their head" enough to be completely in the moment with their body. Athletes and dancers often talk about the state of euphoria they feel when their body and mind are united in an effortless performance. It's a very satisfying feeling that comes without any particular effort to achieve it. It doesn't require *doing* anything in particular: It's a state of being. And it's part and parcel of being an adult.

The goal is to experience the sense of an independent "I" who is the "knower" of your own life. Part of the awkwardness of trying to describe this inmost sense of self is that we're all so focused on the outer qualities or manifestations of a person's identity. If you talk about Bill, you might say that he's this way or that way, he's got this kind of sense of humor, or he's a thinking person more than a feeling person, he's got this shaped body or that color hair, or this way of walking, or these publications to his credit, or drives that kind of car, or loves children and hates cats, or has one disastrous relationship after another, or lives, eats, and drinks baseball.

Certainly all our qualities, habits, and achievements are part of what defines us as individuals. But we're trying to get at something that comes before all that, an unadorned sense of "I"; the "I" that would exist if everyone and everything else in the world disappeared suddenly and there was just this consciousness left, this unique, individual human being. This "proto-I" is the knower of all those facts, the one who exists behind all those facts, the one who moves in and out of external descriptions but is something more than all of them put together.

The Inviolability of Selfhood

Other people's evaluations of us, and their feelings, attitudes, judgments, and thoughts about us in no way alter the reality of who we are. Nor do our opinions alter the reality of anyone else's innermost identity. And yet you wouldn't think this was true, judging by everyone's anxiety about everyone else's opinion. The grownup inside us is caught in the belief that she isn't actually separate from other people: Her sense of self is extremely vulnerable to outside opinion. Unfinished business from childhood has forced her fear and pain around rejection and abandonment into the inaccessible depths of her unconscious. If someone judges her negatively now, or simply doesn't react in a way that feels sufficiently positive, her reaction is one of panic: She feels she has to correct her behavior, appearance, approach, tone of voice—whatever it was that failed to elicit the kind of reaction that would bolster her self-image and sense of value. Because her very identity is threatened, she responds as if this were an emergency.

Someone who had recently connected with her adult self told us, "You can't imagine the difference I feel at work since I no longer take on my boss's panic anytime an order is late." In the past, she had thought that being grown up meant taking responsibility for other people's negative emotions. Her reaction to her boss's panic had always been a Herculean attempt to fix everything and make his negative reactions go away. She had acted in similar ways toward her husband, her mother, and her teenaged children. When things went wrong with them, she always blamed herself; and they, in turn, got in the habit of blaming her, too.

More often than not, we allow other people's judgments, opinions, and feelings to have a strong effect on our perception of who we are. Because of all this outside, extraneous input, our perception of who we are is often very different from who we *really* are. These misperceptions are based in a lack of awareness about the independence of each individual's existence in the world—a lack of contact with the reality, for example, that your boss's or your partner's panic/anger/depression/elation actually has nothing to do with you.

How does this happen that we let the thoughts, feelings, and attitudes of others become more important to us than our own? As children, most of us learned to become extremely sensitive to what our parents reacted to most positively in us. Children use this information in various ways. When they're very young, they'll stand on their heads and spit nickels if this is what seems to delight Mom and Dad. When they're teenagers, they may do exactly the opposite of what they know their parents value, as part of their way of finding a separate identity. In either case, the parents' feelings/perceptions/values are in the foreground. Unless children are encouraged to do otherwise, they have an easy time losing track of what it is that they themselves feel, perceive, and value.

This loss is exacerbated by a general tendency of parents to sweep a lot of children's perceptions and feelings under the rug—to say such things as, "That didn't hurt, darling!" or "Don't be silly—there's nothing to be afraid of!" Kids get the message early on that their own take on reality is untrustworthy. Of course, doubt is a real and valid part of the human condition, whereas self-trust must be taught, reinforced, and encouraged.

Children—and grownups too—need to learn to discriminate between rational and irrational doubt and to recognize when it's a signal that they're out of contact with their internal sense of who they are and what they're being told by their own senses, intelligence, feelings, intuition, and creativity.

When we deny and ignore the fact of our separate interior reality, our interior experience becomes characterized by anxiety. A client related that when she's frightened, she no longer feels the barrier of her skin between herself and the world. She feels in danger both of losing herself—as if the essence of who she is could somehow float away—and of being terribly hurt and violated by people and things on the outside. Understandably, she has trouble going out into the world when she feels this way.

We are especially vulnerable to surrendering our lives to others if our parents haven't given us steady and consistent training in the ownership of self—in other words, by validating our feelings and encouraging us to explore and express them— or training in the exercise of personal power. Such training breeds confidence and a desire to be both independent and fully conscious.

Any parent of a two year old will immediately recognize the thorniness of this territory. It's often necessary in child rearing to place limits on personal power and to teach a child to control his feelings to a certain extent. We don't pretend to have a patent formula that ideally balances these contradictions. Obviously, more work has to be done, and more thinking has to be done.

We do know that people deprived of the validation and encouragement we speak of tend to remain in an unconscious, dependent condition and are inclined to be unresponsive to rational thought or will power in certain areas of their lives. Such people are apt to look for someone or something to idealize and merge with (or, conversely, to trash). In his excellent book about cult behavior, *The Wrong Way Home*, Arthur Deikman calls this state the "dependency dream, [which] acts as an unseen regressive force, shaping our behavior to accomplish the desires of childhood while we are pursuing the goals of adults . . . [The hidden wish] to ride in the back seat of the car has great strength and tenacity. It should be recognized as a permanent part of the human psyche even though in adults it ceases to be as visible as it is in childhood."

My reactions to your expression of your thoughts and feelings are going to be based on the power I think you possess. If, consciously or unconsciously, I believe that what you think of me has the power to determine who I am, I will react to you very differently than I would if I knew that none of your opinions can touch my identity or worth as a human being.

Consider for a moment all the people who set up another person as the ultimate authority in their lives: the boss, the mother or father, the wife or husband, the admired friend, the guru, the mentor. If that authority figure tells an "unseparated" person to lie, falsify records, marry so and so, beat up a competitor, donate money, or hate others, the deed will probably be done, and a rationalization will be found that in no way diminishes the idealized figure's stature.

We interviewed one woman who felt remorse for the harassment and defaming of a competitor she participated in at the instruction of her mentor at work. She explained to us that she had obeyed simply to avoid his "cold look, which told me I was nothing, cutting through to my soul, where I felt like nothing."

Some people have the internal security to say no when asked to do something that falls outside the boundary of what they consider to be moral behavior. They can refuse precisely because they have the integrity or wholeness of a separate sense of themselves. This makes them capable of bearing any consequences resulting from their choice, including loneliness, rejection, and even persecution.

People with a strong internal sense of "I am here"—who know their own value—move in a particular way in the world. In situations where others may be thinking very badly of them, or attacking them verbally, or judging or praising them strongly, they manage to keep a sense of calm within themselves which is also reflected in their activities. The calm isn't a symptom of repression or suppression—these people just know who they are. They know their value and their limitations. They take it on faith that they are seeing their own situation clearly. They believe in the reality of their existence and know that it is rooted solely within them. No one else can touch who they are.

One of our friends put this to practice at her job when she asked for a raise. Her boss agreed that she deserved more pay, but said that she'd have to wait six months before a raise could be put into effect. She told him, "If I'm worth the money then, I'm worth it now." She got her raise right away.

You can see such people move through situations observing, taking care of themselves, making choices, thinking about how they may want to deal with their detractors or their supporters, being very strategic about it, thoughtful about it, strong about it, caring about it, powerful about it. That power comes from some core within them that remains untouched by anyone else's words or attitudes. They experience doubt and fear like everyone else, but they know that these emotions don't define or rule them as individuals. They can experience their feelings without running away from them or being run by them. They can seek solace and reassurance when they need it. They are aware of their grownup training, which labels vulnerability as a cause for shame. They may experience shame. But understanding its source, and the inaccuracy of its judgments, makes them able to experience the emotion without it touching their innermost sense of identity.

Entertaining Ambiguities

The grownup often gets caught in either/or dilemmas: Either I never admit any experience of doubt, and my confidence is unshakable, or I'm overwhelmed with doubt and I feel like a worthless failure. The adult doesn't feel compelled to deny any of the emotions she feels, including negative ones, but her belief in her basic worth is rock solid. There's no possibility that any one emotion—positive or negative—will drastically change her basic belief in herself. Contradictions, paradoxes, and ambiguities can all coexist within the large and generous inner space of her selfhood.

This personal, internal freedom in no way isolates us from the meaning we establish in our lives by being connected to others and making a contribution. When we formed a community group to set up "visioning" meetings to build a plan for the future of our town, there were many times when we experienced doubt and fear that the idea would fall flat. As we encountered each obstacle to the process of setting up the meetings—hostility from inside and outside the group, ignorance, and the agonizing slowness of the process of creating something from scratch—we realized how important it was to constantly reaffirm our intentions and stand behind them, no matter how things were going at any given time.

Sticking with something in the face of adversity requires owning the entire responsibility for what you want to do: No one else will carry out your vision if you give up on it. Paradoxically, it's also essential to be open to the possibility that perhaps your plan isn't the best one out there. It may be that your plan needs to fail so that a better one can take its place.

Grownups can't entertain such ambiguities. Because of their lack of an established and independent sense of self, they are prone to become identified with their project or position to the point where anyone's criticism or expression of doubt translates into a threat to their very identity and sense of self-worth.

We all have this aspect of the grownup within us. The grownup is unconscious of the internal confusion and simply acts it out while telling herself that she just has strong opinions, or that she's "passionate," or that she "didn't care anyway." The adult is conscious of the internal confusion, recognizes the internal signs of this kind of threat, knows that the threat is her problem and not someone else's, and does not have to control, merge with, or dismiss anybody as a way of dealing with it. It's an "inside job" to stay true to yourself while remaining open and related to others in a group.

Here's a simple example of an adult's reaction to a situation that would have daunted a grownup: Karen runs a new local program that collects and distributes food and clothes for migrant workers. She developed the program as soon as she moved into town and saw the need. Her neighbor, a social worker with ties to the migrant community, began to tell people that Karen was on a power trip and that they'd soon see her running for office. Karen never bothered about what her neighbor was saying, because she knew it to be untrue and it didn't have any adverse effect on the project. She told us, "I might make the choice to tell the person that I think she's wrong and let it go at that. But there is really no need to prove anything. I know what is true for me, and I know that the other person is coming from some distorted perception that has nothing to do with me. If she starts to hurt the project, then I may have to take the offensive. We'll see." In fact, Karen was in the process of turning the whole operation over to a committee of farmers' wives so that she could get back to her own work of writing a play.

Permanent Internal Safety

We begin to see how valuable, how critical, the adult self's sense of separateness is in making our way through the world. People who operate by the principle of *I am here, and you are over there* can move through difficult situations, can move through life, with much more safety. Their sense of internal security and value is much greater than that of a person who is ruled by the grownup's operating principle of *I must control, dismiss, or merge with you.* A person without an internal sense of being separate, and the safety and value that come with it, is unnaturally and unnecessarily vulnerable.

A young broker is a case in point. Edward sits in a trading room with another broker next to him. The other broker is a "cowboy" type: He takes more chances and manages his risks much more loosely than Edward, who feels that he too should be as reckless and devil-may-care, especially when he does a deal with this colleague. When he sees a stock go down to a certain level, Edward wants to sell but is embarrassed not to tough it out like the cowboy. In this way, he has often lost money and ended up hating himself.

He sought help, feeling upset that he couldn't honor his own instincts and judgment or trust that his style was as valid as the next man's. He felt threatened by what his colleague thought of him, and admired this man as someone who was "more grown up, more of a man." Because he felt ashamed of his fear, Edward couldn't confront it honestly or with curiosity, and his capacity to learn from his choices was being destroyed.

Edward was able to change this pattern by examining his fear, tracing its sources internally, and taking the very real external chances of trusting his own judgment and learning from his mistakes—which, he was surprised to learn, were not as frequent as he had imagined they would be.

Grownups don't know how to create permanent internal safety for themselves. Attempts to establish a temporary sense of safety can compel us to try to alter the reality of others and ourselves. On an unconscious level inside the grownup, it goes something like this: *I must fix that; I must correct that. I have to correct that either by changing myself, so that you see me differently, or by changing you. I must—it's compelling, it's urgent.*

Most people are familiar with these feelings. We've all dipped if not plunged into this chronic sense of urgency about who we are. Am I okay? Am I acceptable? Am I going to be allowed to be who I am? What are they saying about me? If I show this part of myself, what will happen? When such questions become conscious, their urgency increases. It is as if we are in constant danger of being ourselves. A client of Lou's says that at the end of the day, he meticulously goes over every conversation he has had to see what impression of himself he has created, anxiously noting those impressions he must correct tomorrow. We're not talking about a calm deliberation about what you want to show of yourself, but of that sense of fearfulness that drives you to figure it out before it's too late and you lose.

The emergence of this fearfulness into consciousness is considered a breakdown by the grownup or, at best, a lapse into "foolish childishness" and "weakness." There is shame for feeling this way, as well as a cranking up of defenses to "get it together," to "get a grip." The adult can go another step and hold all of those reactions, including the shame, in an internal, compassionate embrace as a wound from the past—as part of being human, but not as an accurate measure of present reality.

The need to control, merge with, or dismiss another is based in the grownup's unconscious longing for the ideal. We idealize when imperfections threaten us, bringing us in contact with our unhealed wounds. Whether it's a fantasy of the ideal parent, job, relationship, child, friend, or teacher, this concept-on-a-pedestal keeps us from accepting the reality of life. Adults know that life is a mix of good and bad, pleasant and painful—a mix of opposites. No individual is all one way all the time.

You've probably come across people or organizations that give you a taste of the good while promising to get rid of the bad, if you only follow their rules. Ideal behavior supposedly will be rewarded by the ideal. How deeply we believe that the "good" is in the possession of others (rather than residing equally in everyone, including ourselves) determines our ability to maintain our integrity in the face of such promises.

If I know that I exist separately and independently of you—of what you think of me, what you feel about me, your attitudes toward me, that I possess and am responsible for both the good and bad in myself—then whatever you think about me does nothing to alter my internal reality. My knowledge about who I am is unshakable—an intelligent, creative, alive human being. I operate with a sense of self-possession in the world that I wouldn't have without this conviction. I know that I can access both the good and the bad in myself and everything in between—I know that my life is a series of choices.

The grownup's interior reality depends on other people's opinions, judgments, and attitudes. What you think and feel about me can become critical to my existence and my sense of my own value.

This state of awareness that "I am and I exist independently" is a heartfelt feeling. We would describe it as a steady bubble of joy, or a little river of pleasure and excitement running through every day. Again, it's not a big deal. It can expand at times into a very intense experience, but the real pleasure is in the steadiness of it and the sense that it is a given. It's simply a consequence of being alive, unrelated to whether things are going well at a given moment, or whether you're getting what you want, or whether you're being acknowledged in a certain way. Its pleasure resides in the simple fact of being me and being alive. Even if there's something going on that I don't particularly like, or that I strongly dislike, or that causes me pain, I still have a sense of gladness about the "me" existing independently of my pain, disappointment, or frustrations. I'm still myself. I'm still here. I'm still alive, and I'm still consciously experiencing what it means to be me.

There's a quietness to this feeling. The state of awareness has no need to show itself, to exhibit or call attention to itself. It's a very self-contained phenomenon and it's not at all about being isolated or cut off from other people. Quite the contrary—it's a flowing within, but it also flows outward. Ken Wilber, a highly regarded explorer and writer about the realm of internal awareness, puts it this way: "To be a part of a larger whole doesn't mean that the part evaporates. You are an individual, yet you also feel that you are part of the larger unit of a family, which is a larger part of a society."

Harriet Goldhor Lerner, in her book *The Dance of Intimacy*, states that if true, healthy intimacy is to be had, "the goal is to be in relationships where the separate 'I-ness' of both parties can be appreciated and enhanced, and where neither competence nor vulnerability is lost sight of in the self or the other. Intimacy requires a clear self, relentless self-focus, open communication, and a profound respect for differences."

In other words, *I am here, and you are over there.*

Finding the Intimate Witness Inside

Many people have trouble contacting a sense of "I." Try this exercise when you're sitting quietly. Part of the reason why so few of us have the experience of "I" is that we rarely take the time to just be with ourselves without distraction. For a few moments, allow your breath to go in and out at its own pace. Becoming aware of your breathing is a good way to begin contacting a more intimate feeling of who you are. Keep your attention on your breathing. If you find that thoughts interrupt your concentration, gently return to the process of watching your breath. It is your inner "I" that is watching your breathing. It is your inner "I" that is listening to the sounds of your breath. Where is this inner "I" located? Search around inside yourself. Is your awareness located in your heart? Or on your skin? Is it behind your eyes? When you have located what feels like the most vivid location of your essence inside you, stay with it for a while. If your awareness is located behind your eyes, "move" it to your throat. Move the awareness around like a ball of light inside you. Take possession of the different parts of yourself, shedding light in every corner of your being.

Accept your experience of this exercise, whatever it is. It may not "work" for you the first time, and you may want to try it several more times to see if you experience it any differently. There is no right or wrong way. Relaxing and focusing on your breathing will always help you come closer to the sense of "I." In his book, *Wherever You Go, There You Are,* Jon Kabat-Zinn gives some wonderful suggestions on strengthening this internal reality.

CHAPTER FOUR

I Am Safe and Sound Inside My Own Skin

Sticks and stones may break my bones,
but names will never hurt me.
—*Anonymous*

Being solidly grounded in their separate, internal sense of self, adults know that there are no emergencies in life. This is often a shocking statement to grownups, even when it comes with the qualification, "except when health and life are threatened." The "sticks and stones" saying is literally true for adults, who know that their innermost identity and value is immune to verbal attacks—there are no names or words that need be feared.

We remember using this saying as kids in what then felt like feeble attempts to disempower tormentors. Our use of it was more a matter of wishful thinking than conviction—we said it, but we didn't believe that it really did anything to ensure our safety.

We've found that lively debate, puzzlement, or disbelief characteristically follows on the heels of making this "no emergency" statement. Someone always says, "Well, what if you're mugged?" Of course this would constitute an emergency, because it poses a threat to your physical well-being. Others have asked us, "What if someone attacks your character?" or "What if my business takes a downturn?" or "What if I've just separated from my wife, and a guy at work tells me that he saw her out on a date with my best friend?" Such situations can create emergency states inside grownups, but are they in fact real emergencies? Are they really "sticks and stones," or do they have more to do in the end with "names"? If they're not sticks and stones, why do we so often react as though they were? Most of us remain stuck in our childhood "grownup" training, which tells us to avoid at all costs appearing vulnerable or flawed.

In this book, we're using the term *emergency prevention response* to describe a person's efforts to deny, minimize, or dismiss any internal experience—for example, if fear or excitement arises within, and an individual is compelled to say to himself or others, "This feeling has no meaning," or "I'm being foolish," or "Feeling this way is not like me."

The emergency prevention response occurs much more frequently than real emergencies ever do. Most often, it's brought on by something outside the sticks-and-stones category—something that threatens to make conscious the buried fears and vulnerabilities we learned as children to categorize as bad and dangerous. The state of emergency creates an urgent need to answer such questions as: Am I in trouble? Do I count? Am I real? Am I visible? Am I here? What will I lose, what have I lost, what am I losing? The hero in the rock opera *Tommy* repeats the refrain, "See me, feel me, touch me . . ." This is the primal cry of the grownup to the world: "Please do something to convince me of my existence and value!" Our operating principle at these times is *Appearing vulnerable or flawed must always be avoided.* The adult, on the other hand, knows *I am safe and sound inside my own skin.*

Most of us live life in an internal state of muted emergency which can at any time erupt into a full-scale emergency response. We once saw a man at a rather high-brow party react with physical blows when another man criticized his words as being "stupid." Resorting to violence when threatened by words is an extreme example of the emergency response. It can also consist of losing your cool when the maître d' can't seat you immediately, or being bent out of shape by a "funny look" from your date or a colleague at work, or losing sleep over something awkward you said at a party. These would all be trivial matters for the adult self, whose interior sense of value isn't touched by hurtful names, or gestures or errors that imply hurtful names.

You can learn to recognize such responses in yourself by the physical symptoms they produce. It's usually an emergency prevention response if you're experiencing one or more of the following symptoms: shortness of breath; a racing heart; rigidity; an inability to concentrate, hear, focus, or speak clearly; a complete absence of emotions that would be appropriate to the situation, or a tremendously exaggerated response; or a driving need to take action of any kind, regardless of its appropriateness to the situation.

Grownups always have to be at the alert for such emergencies. They already feel shaky about their value and know the urgency of keeping their feelings of worthlessness and insecurity deeply buried, where they can't cause conscious pain. Many people have spent a lifetime submerging their unhealed psychic wounds and they're not about to let a date or a maître d' or someone at a party suddenly bring them to the surface.

There can be a seductive appeal to being involved in emergencies all the time. You probably know people who seem to be in a perpetual state of readiness to rise to any challenge to their authority or sense of being right. These are the aggressive types who blare their horn in traffic or give someone the finger at the drop of a hat. We've seen people at restaurants resort to physical intimidation when it comes time to determine who gets the emotional pay-off of being the one who picks up the tab. Or you may know a blustery type with a lot of power at work who seems to delight in making other people cower. All this braggadocio and its urgency are part of the grownup's attempt to avoid at all cost appearing vulnerable or flawed. Then there are the people who are hypervigilant to rejection or slights or other people's anger—they're the other side of the coin, always ready to withdraw into their own misery and self-loathing. Even though these two types are at opposite ends of the scale, they both reflect a distorted sense of the threat to their identity posed by people's words, gestures, and attitudes.

Operating from a Position of Safety

Far too often in so-called normal discussions among grownups, the overriding concern is not mutual discovery or exploration, but who is right. What might have been a conversation in which differences and ideas were explored becomes an adversarial exchange in which no one hears anyone else or learns anything. Someone comes out the winner, but only at the expense of somebody else coming out the loser.

This is so common and accepted that most of us have come to think of it as normal behavior. We try to outshine others at parties, showing how witty or knowledgeable we are. We start to panic inwardly if a topic comes up about which we're ignorant, or even if someone uses a word whose meaning we don't understand. Rather than taking these situations as opportunities to expand our knowledge, we respond as if the most important thing were to save face. We withdraw when the conversation veers into dangerous territory, or we try to change the subject. If neither of these tactics works, we mentally "trash" the other people involved: They're snobs and eggheads—they know nothing about . . .

Among men, at least, blaring self-confidence, assertiveness, competitiveness, and unshakable opinions are by and large considered to be positive qualities. Women in our society tend to be more concerned about wanting to be liked and needed by others. It's ironic that the very things that can bolster a man's sense of self can cause an emergency in a woman: being referred to as "abrasive" or "a ball buster" or "overly competitive." But, again, these are just opposite sides of the same coin for people who cannot separate from the words and opinions of others.

If physical prowess is most important to us, we are merciless with ourselves when we make mistakes or when our athletic performance somehow falls short of our hopes and expectations. A physical injury can create a complete emergency in someone who relies on his daily workout for his sense of worth and identity.

Being laid up and having to fall back on other resources becomes the equivalent of being left alone and undefended among mortal enemies.

The adult can explore the difference between perceived emergencies and actual ones; the grownup cannot. The ability within grownups to explore the inner state of emergency and check it out with reality is limited by their life-and-death need to never appear vulnerable or flawed. What is important for grownups is to remove any possibility of contact with their internal reality.

As we saw in the previous chapter, grownups flee this contact because of the hurts that overwhelmed them as children which were never acknowledged or healed. So they live in a chronic state of emergency that must nonetheless remain submerged in the unconscious. Part of the effort to keep these feelings submerged involves hiding their vulnerability and flaws, from both themselves and others. Any threat of exposure or pain triggers an emergency prevention response—but the response is actually to the past experience rather than the present one.

Because adults are not in a chronic unconscious state of denied emergency, but rather feel genuinely and deeply safe and sound inside their own skin, they can differentiate more accurately and speedily between real and perceived emergencies. This is true even in the presence of distress generated by the grownup self. If someone or something poses a real threat to life or limb, the adult recognizes this as an emergency and can act accordingly (for example, fighting off or fleeing an attacker).

Adults know that their life does not depend on the approval or acceptance of any other individual or group, that names can never hurt them. They know this not only as an intellectual idea but also as an experienced fact, a state of being, and they rest comfortably and securely in this knowledge. Their identity is safe, valuable, and untouchable. There is no need for defiance; nothing has to be proven or established. There is no need to submit to, or override, other people's opinions and evaluations. It's easy to entertain outside feedback and points of view, because the adult knows that these don't constitute a threat, but rather are simply data.

This doesn't mean that people in contact with their adult self live in a passive state of acceptance, lacking the drive to fight for what they believe in. Rather, they can pick their battles from an inner position of safety and value. For example, no work situation is perceived by the adult to be an emergency, no matter how other people are reacting. There may be an urgency in certain situations—deadlines, a need for speed, a difficult co-worker, even the threat of devastating financial losses. But there's no life-threatening emergency in any of these situations as far as adults are concerned. They know that they can and will do their best and that the rest is out of their control.

As we explore emergency reactions in this chapter, we feel that it's important to remove any judgment from the discussion. Falling into the emergency state, or being driven by the need to prevent contact with it, is not a reason to judge ourselves. Most of us have unhealed wounds and have been raised to be grownups, not adults. We don't arbitrarily make up emergency prevention reactions just to be difficult or ornery. We're only following the models provided by our parents and teachers. More likely than not, we never saw the adult version modeled by our elders, who were themselves taught by their parents, who were taught by *their* parents, and so on. From that perspective, blame becomes a useless tool for dismantling our states of crisis.

Let's say that you have trouble with disagreement. Think about it. In a private argument with your spouse or someone else important to you, what makes it so important that they agree with you, or even concede that your point of view is valid? What's the big deal if they think your point of view is crazy or stupid or poorly thought out? What really is your motivation for pursuing the argument? A love of the truth? A genuine concern for the other person? What is it that pushes us to keep pressing our point home or to have the last word?

It's the fear of being exposed to ourselves and others as wrong or flawed that compels us to win an argument. Being wrong or having our flaws exposed is a conduit to the dreaded feelings of annihilation, abandonment, and shame that we remember or half-remember from childhood—overwhelmingly powerful emergency feelings that we've been trying desperately to keep submerged. It's only in this context that we can understand how a disagreement about who forgot to put the package in the car can become a violent, destructive confrontation.

Taking the adult stance does not mean that we never argue or disagree with anyone. It simply means that we don't confuse the particulars of an argument with the particulars of identity or worth. Being seen as wrong or incompetent, or being defied or ignored, is threatening only if we don't know that we're okay to begin with—if we have no secure place inside ourselves from which to view what's going on in our life.

If we have no secure place inside, other people's challenging behavior makes us feel defensive to the point of not even being able to listen accurately to what's being said. If it feels as though our worth and identity depend on the opinions and reactions of others, we're extremely vulnerable to them; and when they hurt us, we're bound to be enraged. This can be extremely confusing for other people, who probably have no idea what we're reacting to so emotionally. It is only an unusually wise and insightful person who will understand that psychic emergencies of this kind are historical responses to current situations: The pain we're feeling, and trying furiously to bury again, has come out of the past.

Emotional Triggers

What constitutes an emergency is different for different people. Whatever you were shamed for as a child, or whatever occasioned emotional or physical abandonment, will continue to be your emotional triggers. Healing those old wounds and shifting toward the adult state necessitates looking inward and acknowledging the experiences of your inner world that you've tried so hard to keep hidden. If you keep living by grownup rules—for instance, if you live in ignorance of your interior world—you'll never get past the automatic or compulsive responses you learned in childhood and adolescence.

As a defense, grownups sometimes cultivate the opposite behavior from the one that most shamed them in childhood. We know a young man from a verbally abusive family who was himself extremely quiet and nonverbal as a child. There are probably many reasons why he became a lawyer, but the most salient one for us seems to be a driving, unconscious need never to feel vulnerable again in the way he felt as a child. In his field, he's known for his vicious tongue and tenacious desire to win. These qualities bring him success and money at work, but have brought him nothing but failure and pain at home with his fourth wife, troubled children, and friends who know that they must always tread lightly around him if they don't want to get a verbal lashing. If anyone approaches his areas of vulnerability, he is immediately in emergency attack mode. He's a great prosecutor, and he's also a very lonely man with a terrified child inside of him.

Most people will do almost anything to avoid feeling flawed or vulnerable or appearing as such to others. When things fall apart, rather than see our troubles or those of our company or family as a potential growth experience, we react to them as confirmation of our unconscious view of ourselves as worthless. This throws us into emergency mode, dictating behaviors designed for cover-up, coping, and damage control.

Adults have the luxury of seeing problems, mistakes, and changes as opportunities for learning and growth. They don't necessarily like these opportunities any better than grownups do, but they know from past experience that even the most threatening situations can contain the seeds of undreamed-of possibilities and provide a forum for talents they never knew they possessed. Even the most monumental errors of judgment and the most spectacular rejections can produce the chance to experience value in new and wonderful ways. Their perspective is much longer and more leisurely: They know that good things often come about in strange, unexpected, and sometimes painful ways.

Vulnerability

One day, when we were living in a loft in New York City, Fran answered the phone to a gruff male voice that said, "I know where you live and I'm gonna kill you." Without thinking, Fran told him, "Oh, you must have the wrong number," and hung up. It was an experience for Fran of the adult self's spontaneous humor in response to "names" which at another time her grownup might have been all too ready to listen to and believe.

Grownups are constantly reacting out of their fears of being discovered as worthless and flawed. Because they're so stuck in the past, it's difficult for them to react to present situations on their face value. Instead, they're always primed to hear echoes of past hurts in their everyday interactions. Their responses may have little to do with whatever is going on in the present moment, which can be mystifying for other people. When two grownups in the present are interacting out of past griefs, misunderstanding and hurt are bound to prevail. Grownups are emotionally starving for the approval and acceptance they never received as children, but are kept from finding ways of satisfying their hunger because of their belief that appearing flawed or vulnerable will throw them into an emergency situation.

Adults are aware of their need for approval and can readily admit it. They know that if they don't get what they need from other people, it might hurt or feel scary; but they also know that there's no real danger of the sticks-and-stones variety involved. There's no emergency, though there is some sense of vulnerability. Grownups need approval in all its forms, but also feel compelled to deny their need, both to themselves and to others. Vulnerability in itself isn't the problem; rather, the problem is the grownup's compelling need to hide his vulnerability at all costs.

These two conditions—being able to accept flaws and vulnerabilities (because "I am safe and sound inside my own skin"), and feeling compelled to deny flaws and vulnerabilities (because "appearing vulnerable or flawed must always be avoided")—can exist simultaneously within each of us and probably always will to some degree or another. How strong one is in relation to the other, and whether the adult or the grownup dominates a given situation, depends on which buttons are being pushed, how you're feeling on a particular day, how safe you feel with the other person, and so on. It's important to remember that every situation—especially those characterized by conflict—involves all these uncertainties, complexities, and balancing acts for the other person as well as yourself.

Psychic emergencies are the particular domain of the grownup. Let's take a look at a couple of examples of what can transpire when the grownup has the upper hand.

Michael is a successful businessman in his early thirties—ambitious, intelligent, and passionately attached to the car he drives. Every car he has owned has been an extension of his ego.

When he gets into his car (currently a Porsche), it is as if he puts on a new body—the most powerful, good-looking, fastest, best, coolest, most expensive body in town. Many of his feelings of worth are embodied in his car.

Michael drives to work every day. On a typical day, like the one in question, he's cool, he's the king of the road. He's feeling good about himself. Suddenly, in front of him, in the passing lane no less, is a slowpoke. Michael roars up behind him, flashing his lights impatiently. The car doesn't move over; in fact, it seems to slow down. Michael becomes enraged. Now he's blowing his horn and screaming curses at this "idiot" in front of him, who should know better than to be in the passing lane. Michael is in a self-generated emergency. He would not label it as such, but if you look at the intensity and nature of his responses, it's clear that this is a critical situation for him.

When the other car still doesn't move out of his way, Michael whips his Porsche to the right, pulls up alongside the offender's car, and starts screaming out his window. The driver ignores him, which enrages Michael even more. He becomes so preoccupied that he fails to notice the car in front of him slowing down to make a turn until he is practically on top of it. He slams on the brakes, swerves to the right, and skids into some bushes, which scrape the side of his car. Michael is breathing heavily, shaking, unable to control his thoughts. He gets out of the car, sees the damage to his paint job, and feels victimized and enraged all over again. As he proceeds to work, he becomes more and more depressed, and his mood colors his whole day. He tells the people at the office that "some idiot tried to kill me this morning."

This is an example of a grownup being controlled by the distortions of unhealed wounds. We are in trouble from the moment we identify ourselves with our car or any of our possessions. Michael is in trouble from the moment he begins using his car to cover for some unconscious sense of being flawed, imperfect, and vulnerable. His grownup self remains in control all along, even providing a bogus explanation later at work for what happened on the road. As a result of childhood hurts, Michael is burdened by feelings of shame about being dominated and powerless. He has no idea that these wounds persist in him— he has probably never allowed himself to think about the original hurts clearly enough to have much awareness about them. From the moment the other car blocked his path, it became an emergency situation for Michael. His psychic Band-Aid (the car) was ripped off, his wounds were exposed, and defensive rage erupted. In other words, he was forced to reexperience the shameful internal feelings he has spent his grownup life avoiding. Reasserting his power on the road seemed a matter of the utmost importance to him, even more important than the threat he was posing to himself and others by driving recklessly.

Now let's look at Joan, a lawyer in her midforties, married, and about to celebrate her birthday with her husband. She shows up on time at the special restaurant where they'd planned their rendezvous. After she's waited there for an hour, feeling more and more frantic and distressed, the maître d' tells her that her husband has called to say that he'll be delayed. Now all she feels is enraged and insulted. How could Bill be so inconsiderate, especially on her birthday? Why did he wait until she'd been sitting around for a full hour before calling her?

When Bill finally arrives two hours after the appointed time, Joan is too hungry and hurt to listen to his explanation. He tries to coax her out of her sulk as they sit down at the table. "I was in a meeting, sweetheart, that I just couldn't leave until the deal was closed. You know how those things are. Hey, we're both professionals—don't be oversensitive! You know that business comes before pleasure. Now let's forget about the past couple of hours and have ourselves a really nice dinner." Joan relents and tries to have a good time. Later that night, she can't understand why the idea of making love with Bill on her birthday is so repugnant.

Joan's first response was rage at what felt to her like a heartless abandonment by her husband on a night when she needed him. She pretty much hid these feelings from Bill, cued by submerged memories of how expressing rage as a child only provoked more abandoning behavior and rejection on the part of her mom and dad. Joan swallowed her feelings, deferring to her husband's version of what happened and how she was supposed to respond.

The grownup in Joan usually defers to Bill's version of reality rather than experiencing the emergency of expressing her anger. It is one of the underlying reasons why she married Bill in the first place. He cajoles her, or shames her, out of her emergencies. Joan believes Bill when he says that she's oversensitive. She faults herself for being unable to seize the moment. She's afraid that she clings to the past and that she doesn't act like a grownup. Everything Bill has said to her reinforces these fears.

Joan's response to the evening's events was ruled entirely by her grownup self. Her adult self wasn't allowed to respond to perfectly legitimate feelings about the collapse of her evening. None of us gets to preview the intensity, quality, or color of the feelings that may arise at any given time; and adults know that this is okay. As "good" grownups, we try to manipulate our feelings so that they will look or feel more acceptable to ourselves and others. In this way, we create even more layers of garbage to work through before we can get at the truth of our experience. This is the unfavorable position in which the grownup is typically mired. The grownup keeps trying to have someone else's experience; his is never okay, having never been validated in the first place.

Feeling personally diminished, dismissed, or denied is not grounds for emergency responses in an adult. Sure, it can make us feel terrible and provoke us to legitimate anger, but our survival is not really in question, unless we take reckless actions like Michael did. Yet we all have circumstances that are not life-threatening and yet make us feel so panicky that dying, running away, or entering a witness protection program might seem like viable options.

To have responded from her adult self, Joan would have needed to be willing to hold two conflicting sets of feelings at the same time: anger, hurt, and disappointment, and the observant, detached, calm knowledge that her husband is not "the enemy." An adult Joan would know that the situation was not going to become instantly pleasant, no matter what internal shifts she makes. She lets go of any expectations that the evening will somehow revert to her fantasy ideal and puts herself in this new situation, looking around for ways to make it bearable without lying. She will know that there's work to do around the event and that it's going to take time to resolve. She also knows that her relationship with Bill is never going to be quite the same. She needs to hope that nothing has changed, and let that feeling give way to the reality of her hurt, disappointment, and anger at Bill. Allowing such complicated feelings to coexist within her and run their course is not at all easy, but Joan's adult self doesn't flee complexity into the simplistic, narrow solutions that are the grownup's lot.

Sorting Out the Voices Inside You

We can't trust others if we can't trust our own inner experience. In the grownup, all internal experience is suspect. The grownup's defense against feelings of terror and rage is to go back to feeling that it doesn't make sense to trust anyone, including herself. The inner voices say: I told you we'd get hurt . . . You never listen to me . . . It never pays to speak about these feelings—people don't care and don't listen. It's far too easy to revert to an abandoned child's view of the world—hopeless, powerless, and angry.

Most people carry around feelings of despair and hopelessness. In times of stress or conflict, it's hard not to agree with this part of ourselves that is most hurt and damaged emotionally. One of the first things people can do when they decide to be in the adult state is to question the voices inside them and recognize those that are defensive responses left over from the past. If what you're hearing inside makes you feel inadequate, shamed, wrong, incompetent, or despairing, you'd probably be well advised not to trust it as friendly advice, no matter how reasonable and logical it might sound. The adult response is to disempower these voices without shaming the grownup they belong to—after all, the grownup is just trying to cope and is using all the tools he or she has been taught to use.

An important part of getting out of such automatic behavior is letting in its underlying pain. If Michael could become consciously aware of his feelings of vulnerability, he would experience intense pain for a while—but he would also suddenly have choices about how to respond in threatening situations. Without the ability to look inside, he can only act defensively.

The pain is worth it if you no longer have to run away from

what is inside your own skin. You can stand and face what a given person or event on the outside means to you, despite whatever terror and rage you may feel. Adults can do this, because they know that "inside their own skin" is a place of safety.

It's useful to ask yourself a couple of times a day: Who's in charge inside me right now? Is it the adult me, or the unconscious, grownup me? Let your adult self "talk back" to the grownup self who is constantly chattering inside your head. This is good material to practice while you're driving, if you have to drive every day (so long as you're able to drive safely and invent dialogue at the same time!). Here's a sample of some adult "self-talk":

If you stay in charge of our inner experience and keep trying to deny that we feel incompetent, fearful, shameful, and like a failure, or that we expect disaster and have no sense of accomplishment and feel powerless and desperate, then we'll always be focused on those feelings and experiences. We won't be able to step away from them until we can admit them. Denying them means keeping our hands on them to press them down–and having to hold our hands there, never letting go. Life for us won't be an adventure. It'll always feel like a series of near and actual disasters. If you stay in charge internally and don't let me in, this is how it's going to be for the rest of our lives.

I know you're afraid to trust me. But I'm competent and capable. I can learn. I can create. These qualities belong to you too. I'm not going to abandon you. I'm not going to stop listening to the things you say to me or to what you need. I want you to listen to me, to give me some access to our body, our brain, our intuition, so I can use them for both of us, so there'll be a chance of healing our wounds. Even if you won't listen, I'm not going to abandon you. I'll wait until your grip loosens. I want to help us get what we want and need.

Acknowledging the grownup's feeling of emergency—becoming consciously aware of it—is the only way to begin to quell it. The adult must reclaim the power to self-define—not only to know who "me" is, but to reconnect with the self that lives and breathes underneath all the layers of defenses and fears.

Moving more and more toward the awareness that there are no emergencies, that "I am safe and sound inside my own skin," opens a world of discovery and pleasure. Your interior wisdom, as well as your day-to-day potential, becomes more available in terms of its capacity to enrich your life. Everything becomes less and less tense, and more and more fluid; less closed and more open; less automatic and more inventive, intelligent, and spontaneous. You trust yourself, and your trust flows out into a world you can live in safely. The opportunity is suddenly there to love your own life with ardor and curiosity.

Exercise: Practicing Being Safe and Separate

When you have a stretch of time, sit down quietly with a notebook. Put one of these headings on each of four different pages: *What Happened, What I Think, What I Think They Think,* and *What They Think.* Now recall an event that made you feel really uncomfortable. Under the first heading, describe in great detail what happened—facts only, no interpretation. What happened? Who said what to whom? What actions were taken? On the second page, record what you think happened, including your feelings, interpretations, thoughts, and judgments about the event. On the next page, imagine in vivid detail what the other people involved thought about the event and all the people involved (include your assessment of their analysis, judgments, and feelings, too). Write all of this down. If you feel safe enough, at the next opportunity, ask the others involved for their reactions—what they think happened. Write down or record what they actually tell you—this is information for the fourth sheet of paper. After each thing they tell you, rephrase it and tell it back to them. Ask them, "Is that what you said?"

At no time in this process are you to question your own or the other person's experience. You simply accept what is said to you as being true for the person who says it. After you have gathered the information for each heading, compare what is real for you with what they have told you is real for them. Separate out what you imagined from what they told you was their experience. If you get upset that there are areas of disagreement, note where in the story your upset occurs. The degree to which you are separate from those people is the degree to which you can accept their version of events as being real for them, even when they don't accord with your own version of reality.

A client of Lou's said after doing this exercise, "I know what I saw. How could they possibly have seen the opposite? I don't like it, but I'm obviously going to have to expand to fit this." Practicing to have a solid sense of "I," knowing you are safe inside, you can expand your consciousness to include more and more of life, becoming less fearful and judgmental about how others think and live. That doesn't mean that you have to abandon your own perspective and accept everyone else's version of reality, but it does mean that you can be flexible and stay in open communication with yourself and others.

CHAPTER FIVE

CHAPTER FIVE

I Am Curious About Everything That Goes On Inside Me

"In the modern world, the cruelest thing that you can do to people is to make them ashamed of their complexity."

— Leon Wieseltier

Adults are able to be aware of virtually any interior experience without shying away from it. They can tolerate the thoughts of revenge, scandalous fantasies, and agonizing emotions that a grownup would have to stuff down and censor as quickly as possible to avert a psychic emergency. For the conscious adult, even the most shadowy and terrifying realizations about the self are an occasion for further probing. Adults never lose their curiosity about who they are and how that self is manifested. To be able to plumb the depths of your self, and find the hidden treasures buried inside, you have to be willing to encounter both the light and the dark sides of your personality, history, memories, and motivations.

The interior place where such encounters occur marks the borderline between the grownup and the adult. It is here where grownups feel compelled to avert their eyes, turn out the lights, and stop exploring. The grownup's operating principle when confronted with his own darkness is *I pay attention only to "reality."*

In *The Road Less Traveled,* author and psychiatrist M. Scott Peck writes that at the beginning of his work with a new patient, he draws a circle with a small wedge in it. He tells his new client that 95 percent of the circle represents an individual's unconscious mind, while the little wedge represents the part of us that we consciously experience. The more we learn about that 95 percent, the more we will belong to ourselves, be truly and effectively tapped into our life, and have a say about it.

The unknown is terrifying to people who lived in environments hostile to their interior development when they were young. And it continues to terrify them in later life if they fail to look within that interior world to find, accept, and understand the buried causes of their fear. The internal unknown is a vital part of life, delivering both pleasant and unpleasant surprises and holding both empowering and devastating information, which can be integrated or divested with time and care.

What occurs on the surface of life often has little to do with what really moves us. This applies to our hidden negative motivations and beliefs, as well as to our deeper capacities for creativity, awareness, and love. The full truth of our lives evolves from a profound interior level. C. G. Jung said that what we don't become conscious of we are destined to live out as fate. Living things out as fate can be very painful, like traveling the Himalayas using a map of New York City for guidance, when you aren't even sure you agreed to go on the trek in the first place.

Years ago, when Fran was running for the school board, she volunteered to take the pictures of all the local candidates to be displayed at the election site. She had the pictures developed the day they were due to be displayed. "I noticed vaguely that the picture of my opponent was missing, but didn't feel any undue anxiety about it—I just told myself that it was too bad it didn't print. The looks I got after the pictures were displayed didn't do anything to penetrate my unconscious competitiveness either.

When, days later, I realized what I had done, I was truly ashamed and in awe of the power of the unconscious. What I had done had been so obvious to everyone but me."

The power of denial, as they say in twelve-step-program circles, is awesome. What they're talking about is the power of the *need* to be unconscious. Fran's competitive feelings weren't bad in and of themselves. The problem was her need to hide them. "I had learned as a child that competitiveness was bad. Any such feelings I had went automatically underground, where they were completely inaccessible to my conscious awareness.

"After the election, which I lost, I had no way of integrating the new information into my life. Instead, because the shame was too painful to bear, it became critical for me to change people's perception of me as someone who was deceptively competitive. I also tried to forget about the incident, telling myself that it was an isolated mistake and that I'd just have to pay more attention to detail in the future. I had no understanding of my need to win or my ambivalence about being of service. In short, I had no understanding of the unconscious emotions that were significantly influencing my daily life. But this kind of behavior was not isolated and continued to plague me. That my behavior was controlled by an emotionally wounded part of me was the farthest thing from my awareness."

Lou remembers the experience that started his personal awakening process. "I had just started psychotherapy. In my first session, the therapist pointed out something about me that I considered a bad trait: that I seemed preoccupied with judging myself and others. I had never thought of myself that way and was shocked that he said such a thing. When it came time for my second session, I left my office to go to the therapist's office; unaware of even the slightest ambivalence about going, I went right past the stop on the bus and then proceeded to walk past his street. Realizing my error, I corrected myself, only to walk past his building, correct myself again, and then take a wrong turn out of the elevator so I was headed down the hallway *away* from his office!

"By the time I got to his door, I knew in my gut that I unconsciously did not want to be there. It was tempting to just write it off as symptomatic of being mixed-up, tired, or spaced out, but the recognition was too loud and clear about what was happening. This was my first experiential knowledge of something in me, which I was not initially aware of, that was actively influencing my behavior. That recognition was the beginning of an adult response to my own unconscious."

The adult in Lou was able to tolerate the knowledge of his resistance, the cause of it, and the difficult steps necessary to continue dismantling it. Our adult values are not the same as our grownup values. Adults are aware that they live with both sets of values all the time. The adult wants to know what goes on inside himself strongly enough to tolerate intense discomfort while finding out, whereas the grownup seeks emergency relief through continued avoidance of contact with his own insides. Lou's adult self knew that the wounded, grownup part of him would continue to resist seeing and changing—that he was divided within. This was part of the information conferred by the incident, and part of what he had to accept. It is part of what all adults come to accept.

Claiming Your Unconscious

The discovery of the personal unconscious is a transforming event. Once you are aware that you live with emotions, beliefs, attitudes, and self-conceptions that are beyond your normal waking consciousness, your relationship to yourself, to others, and to the world is fundamentally changed. Life is no longer quite so simple, yet, at the same time, certain mysteries are clarified. You can no longer blithely assume that what you are conscious of about yourself and others constitutes the whole truth.

When you know that you have an active and influential unconscious, you can give serious consideration to what other people say about you. You can no longer assume that anyone criticizing your words or behavior is either overcritical, dysfunctional, or simply wrong. Of course, such people may be wrong, but you can no longer refuse to pay attention, because you know that your unconscious plays a part in everything you do and say—and it might be trying to tell you something.

For example, if what I am conscious of is that I like and value myself, but yet I fail to take good physical care of myself, there's obviously something else going on. These splits between our ideas about ourselves and our actuality provide the openings for consciousness to penetrate. Adults do not see the unknown as the enemy, but welcome these openings for the information they offer us about ourselves. In our training to be good grownups, we are taught to be honest, but also to do everything in our power to stay unconscious internally, ignoring gut feelings, intuition, feedback about discrepancies in our values and behavior, and the evidence in front of our eyes that tells us that something is not as it should be.

Personal awareness of the unconscious has tremendous social implications. It raises the question of honesty in all our relationships. To call the grownup's lack of awareness "lying" is judgmental and counterproductive. Because until we become aware, real choice is unavailable to us. We have a choice only when we are conscious of having a choice. Adults accept the gaps in their consciousness as a forgivable part of their own humanity and are prepared to make reparation to themselves and others for the harms unconsciously wrought.

If the accuracy of your self-perception turns out not to be as trustworthy as you thought it was, you're presented with a choice: You can go back to blissful ignorance; or you can choose to be more open—to question and explore your words, actions, and feelings more than you've ever done before.

Such a decision strips away our defensive arrogance and requires an adult fearlessness in the face of the unknown. We experience a loss of innocence. The wounded child in us wants to run away and deny the fearful truths. If the adult prevails, remains, and reflects, the experience of turning within can lead to more compassion and understanding for ourselves and others. It becomes possible for kindness to become a real part of our external and internal interactions. Apologies become opportunities to repair connections rather than be the dreaded necessities they so often are. We might better understand our connection with others and consider their comfort as carefully as we consider our own. Seen from this new perspective, the tension in the office with a particular person could be relieved, or an opinion we hold righteously could be reformulated with our partner and our relationship eased. To have this effect, the awareness of a personal unconscious must be a heartfelt experience, not just an intellectual acknowledgment.

The grownup part of us is completely comfortable with intellectual rationalizations. They are like bedtime stories that allow us to fall into an unconscious sleep and require no integration into real life. For example, there is a man on one of the boards in our town who is abusively insulting and arrogant with people, even though he has good suggestions to make. He doesn't understand the effect he has on others. Many people have told him their feelings about his behavior, but he laughs them off, satisfied with his own view that people appreciate his straightforward manner. Really taking in what other people have to say about him would send him into a psychic emergency. He needs to keep his dark qualities—his "shadow"—completely outside his conscious awareness in order to feel that he can function from day to day.

The Shadow Knows

Your "shadow" contains everything you had to bury as a youngster because you were given the message that it was unacceptable. The veiled nastiness of the local politician described previously, Fran's unconscious competitiveness, Lou's tendency to be judgmental—all these are examples of shadow qualities that people may feel compelled to deny. Your shadow can hide positive as well as negative characteristics. The Reverend Martin Luther King Jr. understood this when he said, "Man is neither villain nor hero: he is rather both villain and hero." Joy, success, a sense of humor, and a sense of pride in oneself are some of the things children are sometimes forced to disown and hide in the shadow, right alongside their rage, envy, aggression, sadness, and all the rest of the traditionally negative emotions.

Your shadow might include qualities that anyone would feel glad to possess: ambition, excitement, sensitivity, compassion, artistic vision. But when a wounded grownup is in charge of your life, these qualities have to stay buried, just as they did when, for one reason or another, they posed a threat to your family. The adult in you is capable of excavating them, because the adult is not afraid of seeing and claiming either your deficits or your power, and no longer believes that seeing is dangerous in the way it was in the past. But until the adult part of you takes the upper hand, your shadow qualities will have to stay hidden from conscious view. In their book, *Primary Speech: A Psychology of Prayer,* Ann and Barry Ulanov write: "Our best parts, if left unlived, can be as poisonous as our worst, if left unhealed."

It's not uncommon for your own buried feelings and qualities to show themselves to you in other people. This is called projection, and it can be very difficult to sort out from real life. People project both positive and negative qualities onto others. What we fear in ourselves, we idolize or demonize in others. When two grownups are interacting, there may be so much projection going on—with so little awareness—that each individual is holding a sort of monologue with a blank screen. No meaningful communication occurs, and the situation is a hotbed for misunderstanding and hurt feelings. When, for example, you can't own your own aggressive energies and feelings, you lose a source of strength and protection and transfer that power to another. The Ulanovs address this in their book as well: "Oversensitivity to being hurt turns up. This is not caused by our delicate nature but by the refusal to use our own aggression, forcing it then to turn against us as it inflates the slightest criticism into an all-out attack that levels us. We endow others with our own unlived aggression."

Your shadow contains all the parts of your personality that were whittled away for survival value and replaced by an acceptable public image. You can find the needy one there, the angry one, the one who was too smart for her own good, the terrified one, the seductive one, the fearless risk-taker, and the abandoned child. There is an endless range of personality traits and behaviors that may have threatened your parents and grandparents, your siblings, your teachers, your schoolmates, and maybe even your ancestors (if family members among the living were to be believed). You had to get rid of those qualities to survive, either physically or emotionally or both.

The shame of having to hide aspects of yourself stunts the growth of your sense of value. Sometimes, even for those people who function well in their outer lives, the inner world is a cold and empty place, shuttered and locked. Why go into such forbidding and uncomfortable territory? Locked away there are the disowned pieces of your identity, which surface every now and then in moments of confusion or at times when you realize you have no idea what you want or what you believe.

For the most part in our society, these inner stirrings are treated as things to get over, to medicate, to feel embarrassed about. But it is in turning your gaze inward and beginning to walk this interior domain that you free yourself from inner isolation, confusion, emptiness, and meaninglessness. It is only here that you can reclaim your lost abilities and capacity for experience and feeling. This is your treasure hoard, and it is unlike anyone else's.

Qualities you're glad to reclaim from the shadow realm can cause you fear and anxiety as they begin to emerge. No matter how great it is to feel the joy or competence once hidden from you, in the beginning they may be tainted by the presence of the fear and anxiety that relegated them underground in the first place. When you resurrect a piece of yourself, the whole complex of feeling, memory, defense, and requirement surrounding the burial of a given quality emerges into consciousness with it. As a friend put it, "I am doing something good for myself. So how come I feel like shit?"

This muddled state of limbo is one you have to recognize and pass through on your path to a conscious life. But it's far better to experience this interim discomfort than to live in the numbed state of unconsciousness in which your defenses run you, and you never claim the freedom and richness lying dormant inside you.

The simplest things—deciding to go to the movies, realizing that you like one friend better than another—are decisions made inside you before and beneath your conscious awareness of them. The interplay of ideas, thoughts, and emotions in the unconscious colors all the decisions you make from day to day, whether you pay attention to that reality or not.

Grownups have a superficial relationship to their interior life, barely listening to its information, prompts, or comments. For the adult, this relationship is rich and intimate, a series of deeply felt, conscious interludes. In this process, adults are continuously discovering and being surprised by who they are.

Initially, when adults-in-the-making spend time contacting their inner resources, they tend to hope that the contact will bring solutions to their problems or answers to their questions about why they feel stuck. Curiously enough, as you keep looking inward, your focus shifts from wanting relief to a simple interest in the growth and communication going on inside you. There can be a tremendous sense of relief in recognizing that this process, these voices, and this learning are *yours:* your inner life is the truest mirror you'll ever find. It is here that you can feel a sense of connection, wholeness, acceptance, and peace. Some of the methods of going deeper are reflection, contemplation, prayer, meditation, psychotherapy, consultation, friendship, silence, and creative work.

Delving into the Pit

Delving into the negative unconscious is the grownup's rite of passage into conscious adulthood. Like all rites of passage, it is both difficult and dangerous. In describing the pain of this experience, we have often spoken of it as being in "the pit." Surviving the pit entails successfully confronting things you've buried in your unconscious: the experience of feeling useless, unworthy, violent, imperfect, lazy, hopeless, deceitful, doubtful, isolated, and wrong, a disappointment to yourself and others. When you're in the pit, it can feel as though this is the "real" you—the one you've been afraid of, and running from, all these years.

The pit is a pain-filled place buried inside, where neither reassurance nor palliatives can reach. It is where you are forced to touch your unhealed wounds with whatever love and compassion you can muster. We all get there at some point in our lives, whether we take small peeks now and then when we're feeling low, or suffer a tremendous blow that sends us plummeting to its depths completely without warning. You can arrange your own descent to the pit, or life and circumstances can send you there on their own accord. Knowing about this is not it. Being in it is. We're talking about an experience of total darkness and abandonment in which your most cherished beliefs, ideas, needs, and dreams are destroyed or so mutilated that your life is knocked completely off balance.

For some, the experience of the pit is brief; for others, it is a lifelong intermittent process. It may be tied to a painful event and never experienced outside of that context. Some of us go through it once; others go through it again and again, watching its power diminish over time. The experience is always painful, and always contains the things you most hate to deal with. Even if you expect pain in life, the pit is often much worse than any pain you've ever imagined. The disillusionment when you glimpse the real motivations behind your actions, the betrayal or abandonment by someone you trusted completely, the sudden and inexplicable illness that threatens to rob you of everything, the death of someone dear to you, the death of a cherished dream—any such realizations or events can catapult you unexpectedly into the realm of your inner shadow. In David Rosenbaum's novel *Zaddik*, a seer asks a wise man, "How can we take such a terrible step when we are not sure?" The wise man answers, "We leap into darkness because the fire rages at our backs."

Pain is probably one of the few sensations that cuts through unconsciousness at top speed. When we are trained to pay no attention to pain, especially inner pain, we miss its message and, as a result, experience more pain.

Pain and discomfort are powerful sources of information in the hands of an adult. Fran comments, "In time, the need to find meaning in my life, a life in which pain had played such a large role, motivated me to look inside at my embarrassing behavior and, instead of judging it, to learn what was really behind it." This process of looking is a tug-of-war between the reluctant grownup and the seeking adult.

Most grownups view pain as something to alleviate as quickly as possible. They see it as a flaw, a sign of weakness or failure. Adults also want to get rid of their pain, but they know they may have to experience it for a while if they're to learn from it, and they're not ashamed of its presence. They pay attention to their pain and learn from it as a consequence. It is in looking for insight from a painful situation that the beginnings of adult consciousness begin to dawn.

Part of becoming an adult means exercising the ability to step back and look inside at what is happening, instead of being caught in the swirl of emergency prevention responses. A way to begin learning this is to practice looking at events from within the separateness and safety of your inner being. For example, when someone criticizes another person's work, habits, or parenting style, you can ask yourself: What's the real content of the criticism? Does it seem to be justified? Do I agree with what's being said? Does it come out of the critic's envy or sense of competitiveness? By making me party to this criticism of someone else, is the critic trying to form an alliance with me, or pay a compliment to me, or warn me that I might be next up for dissection when he/she is talking with someone else?

In other words, take an event and expand your awareness of it. It's very likely that most of your questions won't have definite answers. The important thing is to question, not to have the answers. When someone comes at you with rage or anger, step back and know that the rage belongs to them. It is not yours, and you don't have to be angry in return. When someone hurts you, feel the hurt, and see what it has to tell you. Step back and ask yourself what this has to do with you, and if this is not in reality more about the one who has been hurtful than about you. It still may hurt, but now you can make choices. Practice this with other people's effects on you, and soon you'll be able to be equally open-minded about the effects of your own words and behavior on others.

Learning to Know and Accept All the Parts That Make the Whole

A crucial aspect of the process of waking up is to accept and own all the internal experiences that make us who we are, even those that are painful, irrational, embarrassing, self-hating, and resistant to change. No matter how something got into you, it's your responsibility to take care of it now. Beating yourself up, yelling, shaming, or denying that part of you only reinforces it, and will make it hard to keep the painful quality in your conscious awareness, where you at least have a chance of dealing with it. Going unconscious is one of our last defenses when faced with pain we have no tools to deal with. Unfortunately, the unconscious has only one exit—the one leading through our conscious awareness. Anything that doesn't go this route is stuck inside, where it can grow and fester and continue to do harm by limiting us unnecessarily, taking the color and richness out of our lives, or blinding us to the harm or good we do.

Instead of going unconscious, you can behave with your distressed and resistant grownup as you would with a child. You have to stop what you're doing and pay attention to what is being communicated. There is an exercise at the end of this chapter to help you with this.

This is a good place to mention dreams. Dreams are a link between that 95 percent of our consciousness that is inaccessible and the tiny wedge we think of as running the show. They can tell us the real story of what is unfolding in our lives. One client told Lou why she loves the information she gets from her dreams: "I can't manipulate it. My will has nothing to do with what is presented or explained. They are a source I can finally trust. In some mysterious way, that's me talking to me." Dreams bypass rationalization, absence of feeling, good sense, manners, and moral codes to bring us core information about ourselves. This is why the grownup, whose focus is exclusively on external reality, pays no attention to them. Understanding your dreams and the messages they hold takes practice, attention, and usually help from someone who has had a lot of experience helping other people remember and interpret their dreams. There are several texts that can help you access and interpret your dreams. We especially recommend C. G. Jung's *Memories, Dreams, Reflections* and Dr. Frederick S. Perls' *Gestalt Therapy Verbatim*.

Besides the traces it leaves in our dreams and on the events of our daily lives, our unconscious shadow also appears in the stories and ideas we were raised on. We all carry both negative and positive family stories in our unconscious, and the grownup believes them absolutely and without question. Fran relates, "While I was talking to our daughter, explaining to her why things are so often unfair, she interrupted me by saying, 'I don't want your world view.' I had been speaking with great love to her—this rejection of all I had to say was sudden and unwanted. The vulnerable child in me tried to dive down and shut off what she was saying. All these grownup phrases like, 'You'll learn,' and 'Don't be disrespectful!' bubbled up inside me. But I have learned to wait for my adult voice, so I kept my mouth shut and listened carefully until a light went on in my brain.

"The stories I tell myself about life—even about how unfair life sometimes is—are vehicles for my unconscious material. In my narrow vision, how I saw life was the only way to see it—an amalgam of family, social, and psychic needs formed by my past. Here was my daughter, refusing to accept my version of the story for her own life. As I allowed myself to hear that 'no,' it became conscious for me that my view was only one of many and that I could choose to change it. My truth, learned from my family, was as much a story as any you could find in the fiction section of the library."

Family stories are so potent—and so hard to sort out from objective truth—because we're fed them almost as food from the very beginning of our lives. A man may grow up "knowing" that he can never excel in any career because of a family tradition of men who felt frustrated and unfulfilled. Or a woman might accept one bad relationship after another because unsatisfying relationships between men and women were all she ever saw. One of the people who talked to us about family stories put it this way: "I know that even my suicidal thoughts are not truly my own. I am carrying my mother's guilty wish to die because her birth was the cause of her mother's death. Neither of us needs to die. My grandmother died of what was then called childbed fever. The original pain of that event has never been handled or acknowledged in my mother's family. My mother carried the pain, guilt, and anger about that event which orphaned her and her seven brothers and sisters. She was the scapegoat, and she unloaded the emotional burden of that role in the way she acted and viewed life. Her negation of self was passed along the shadowy unconscious pathways of her life to my life."

When you've brought to light some of your family myths, as well as the beliefs they've created in you, it's of great help to acknowledge your independence in the world—*I am here, and you are over there.* When you know that you exist independently of everyone else, both living and dead, you can begin to make independent decisions. You're no longer obligated to live out your family stories. They are still part of who you are, and always will be, but it's in your interest to find those aspects of them that can give you strength, rather than let yourself be frustrated by those aspects that limit you or rob you of your potential.

In this chapter, we've stressed some of the hard truths that are the adult's lot. But your unconscious also harbors hidden joys, power, and meaning. Whatever you, your parents, your teachers, and society didn't want you to be is there inside you, waiting to be discovered like treasures in an attic. This chapter is about exposing and vanquishing whatever ghosts haunt your inner house and keep you from exploring the attic. The following chapters are about some of the treasures awaiting you there.

Reclaiming What Belongs to You

This exercise can tell you where you stand with regard to a quality you may have projected onto someone else. Write, or speak into a tape recorder, describing a quality or trait you admire or detest in another person. Be very detailed in your description of the trait. Can you have it? Or is it something you could never accommodate in your identity as you know it now? Now change places with that person, feeling and having the admired (or detested) characteristic yourself. What is it like to be this way? Does the quality manifest itself differently in you than it does in the other person? Is it more or less positive or negative in you? Can you do things you were never able to do before you allowed yourself to possess or reclaim this quality? Are you still the same person you were before? How are you different? What aspects of your life would you need to modify, and what beliefs, assumptions, and ideas would you have to give up, in order to continue to possess this quality—to hang on to it forever? You can use this exercise to reclaim any parts of yourself you were forced to give away because they made other people uncomfortable, or made you feel ashamed or afraid of being abandoned.

CHAPTER SIX

I Learn from My Emotions

*"Emotion is the chief source of all becoming-consciousness.
There can be no transforming of darkness into light or of apathy
into movement without emotion."*

–Carl Gustav Jung

We heard a story from a young woman about an evening she spent at a Chinese restaurant with some friends. They were seated at a table toward the rear of the room, enjoying their meal, when cooks and waiters suddenly came pouring out of the kitchen. Getting a glimpse through the kitchen door from where she sat, the woman saw that the walls were in flames. Frightened, she told her friends that they'd better get out of the restaurant—the whole kitchen was on fire. One of the men laughed and told her, "Oh, they're always having grease-fires in this place. The cooks always panic, but it's never anything serious." Unable to get her friends to pay any attention at all to the danger she perceived, the young woman told them she was leaving, and made her way as quickly as she could out the front door. Her companions were the last to get out of the restaurant, and all wound up suffering from smoke inhalation.

When you know that you exist and are safe within your own personal boundaries, it becomes possible to look at your emotions as vital sources of information, meaning, and vitality. In telling us her story, the young woman commented that she might have acted very differently in her "grownup" past. Like her companions, she would have needed to appear in control of her emotions and would have tried to talk herself out of her fear.

If you have no fear, or if you don't allow your fears to affect you, you can put yourself in very real danger. Similarly, if you have no anger, it becomes possible to live with a person who abuses you or your children. If you have no real joy in your life, you can be comfortable thinking about your death, even wishing for it.

Be cool! and *chill out!* are modern bywords not only for youngsters, but for grownups who have been trained to shut down the information coming from their senses. Grownups believe that they should be above their emotions, always able to master them. Most people are so afraid of being overwhelmed by their feelings that they go to great lengths to keep them in check. In the process, they often dull or destroy their ability to feel things deeply.

Good grownups are very cool all the time. Look at our almost universal cultural admiration for the British, those inventors of the "stiff upper lip"! Complete *sang-froid*—literally, "cold blood"—is the ultimate protection against experiencing the hidden surprises that can boil up at any time in the course of ordinary events. The relevant grownup operating principle or governing idea is *I must control my emotions at all times.*

Look at a young child's emotional responses to the world, and then look at those of the so-called adults around you. Granted, we wouldn't all want to maintain quite the emotional intensity of two year olds—but it does seem that we lose out on a lot of our potential, especially our potential for delight. In the microcosm of evolution in each human being, the ability to feel joy becomes as impaired and faded as the sense of smell in modern humankind. Our ability now is a mere trace of the sensory capacity we once possessed.

Strong emotions can threaten the image of ourselves we construct so carefully, both for public consumption and the person we see every morning in the bathroom mirror. It can feel as though strong emotions will render you as powerless as you were when you were two years old and uninhibited. Many grownups regard emotionality as unnecessarily time-consuming—an annoying digression from rational thought and the real business of life (whatever that is).

Suppressing our emotions allows us to float above potential hurt, humiliation, or pain, but the resulting loss of information can be critical (as in the example involving the Chinese restaurant). Not only do you lose out on information, but a lot of the nuances of life—and the beauty—simply can't thrive in the arctic temperatures of the grownup's ultracool world.

Adults cultivate an inner sense of calm and stability that does not require giving up either the information or the spice carried by strong feelings. The relevant operating principle for the adult is *I learn from my emotions.*

The Emotional Banquet

When we're taught to grow up rather than allowed to mature, we respond inwardly to our emotions by ignoring, denying, minimizing, manipulating, intellectualizing, and needing to be "right" about them. Emotions are deeply personal and subjective; they run counter to the grownup's need to conform to fixed models. On the other hand, adults who have been allowed to mature listen to what their emotions are telling them, trust that information as real, probe and experiment with it, savor it, and share it with others. Emotions are just emotions, but how we react to them internally determines what, if anything, we're able to learn from them. Our internal relationship to them constitutes the difference between an adult and a grownup response.

The adult is aware of the emotional binds in which the grownup lives. The grownup is trained to view emotions negatively. At their first appearance, his energy is unconsciously and automatically geared to shutting them down and controlling the fear they cause him. Emotions end up being emergencies, and the grownup begins whatever emergency prevention responses he has learned. Every emotional situation becomes tense, whether or not it is inherently so. The grownup doesn't get to experience the emotion—or learn what it has to teach him—but he suffers the emergency anyway. Denying feelings splits your energy and binds you to a state in which you never know what is really true about yourself or your situation.

A dearth of feeling can impoverish even the richest of lives. We know a successful businessman, who threw a "retirement" party for an aspect of himself he called "the zoner." For him, that name covered his experience of moving through life with skill and success but very little feeling. "The zoner did everything compulsively and with consummate skill—but I wasn't allowed to be present emotionally to claim any part of the experience. It might as well have been somebody else's life I was living." Without the richness conferred by deep feeling, life becomes shallow and narrow and meaningless.

Not caring is a way of insulating ourselves against being hurt all over again in the ways in which we were hurt as undefended children. We "feel" our emotions only in safe and approved ways—perhaps we cry at the movies, or get emotionally involved in a book or a television program, or get choked up during tear-jerker commercials, or cry at funerals. But when it comes to consciously experiencing what we feel about the people closest to us while they're living, or the miraculous joy of simply being alive and on this planet, we stuff our emotions away and out of sight, even out of mind. To know love is to fear loss. To claim your anger is to explore the prospect of being separate and alone. To know the true joy of being alive is to experience the certainty of death. Most people don't feel strong enough to allow themselves to be so vulnerable. So they swallow their love, fear, anger, and joy, and settle for merely surviving and feeling safe.

This neutral ground provides a defense against the freely expressed preferences and personal choices that we've come to associate with punishment and feelings of shame. The emotions that by rights should define our adulthood come to be seen as weak spots in our character that need to be excised.

Some of us have done such an effective grownup job of eliminating and manipulating our emotions that we go through life feeling very little. All that would define our personal uniqueness is buried, and nothing stands out or appears remarkable in the world around us. All children seem the same, all trees look alike, snow is only snow, rain is only rain; all birthdays and holidays provoke feelings of guilt, inadequacy, and disappointment. Love boils down to sex or obligation. Friendship is fleeting, and is largely about using people to get where you want to go. Work becomes a ball-and-chain. So does marriage.

These are the outcomes of the very grownup behavior of repressing our emotions. It's like losing your sense of taste and smell and then chewing your way joylessly through life's banquet. You won't starve to death . . . but, oh, what you're missing!

The well-trained grownup says, "I will talk only about ideas

—
119

with you. I will never tell you how I feel about them or how they affect me, nor do I want to know how you feel about anything." A very successful performing artist we know confided in us, "I was so successful; I made money and had lots of people interested in me and in my work. It wasn't cool to care about anything like that, so while it was happening I pretended not to notice or be excited. I was very sophisticated and bored with it all. The pendulum has swung the other way now, and I missed all the fun and excitement of that kind of success when I had it."

This same deadening of feeling was described by a neighbor of ours: "My daughter is gone now, moved to the coast. She never calls. I thought it would bother me, but it doesn't. You see, we had a very businesslike relationship. I had very high standards for her, and she was very obedient. I don't know what her favorite colors are, or why she had chosen to be a vegetarian. I don't know why she stopped playing basketball when she was twelve, even though she seemed to like it. I never thought to ask. It didn't seem important at the time, and now she says she doesn't remember. Perhaps I taught her to ignore her feelings, too."

The adult can revel in emotions that inspire creativity and positive change, that carry a charge of courage and determination. Without such feelings, even what we choose to do becomes burdensome. Meaning is sapped from our lives when our emotional motivation is killed or crippled. So many grownups experience an absence of meaning in their lives because they don't feel safe enough internally to embrace their own feelings.

Emotions are especially threatening when they become obsessive, occurring over and over again and feeling completely out of control. Rather than listen to such emotions for the information they convey, grownups put all their effort into trying to make the emotions stop. In this situation, emotions assume a power they were never meant to have. An emotion has no need to repeat itself over and over again unless we are ignoring its message. The physical parallel would be getting the cue from your body that you're hungry, but failing to eat; or feeling cold but not putting on warmer clothes.

In war, the repetition of fear is a normal reaction. Feeling sad each time you visit a relative in the hospital is a normal reaction. But repetitive, chronic anxiety, depression, rage, shame, or obsessive thoughts are the results of destructive early childhood training and blocked emotional growth (barring a physiological disorder). Under open and safe conditions, emotions emerge within us and prompt us to action and expression. When the emotion is acknowledged, examined for information, and responded to appropriately, its cycle is finished and it goes away.

A More Effective Relationship to Emotion

Grownups who have had to shut down emotionally are forced to look outside themselves for cues about how they should feel. They may look to their partner to supply the emotional content of their life; or they may surround themselves with authority figures to whom they can refer all aspects of their lives for answers, judgment, and approval. These are the people who need to stay in destructive family situations rather than leave, or who may be the support behind charismatic but corrupt leaders. They also provide fodder for cults. At the extreme, they may be so disconnected and so hurt that they resort to violence against people who see through their defensive shell to the vulnerable person inside. Killing or dying, in such extreme cases, can seem preferable to being exposed to the possibility of feeling one's full burden of pain.

Emotions are one of the ways in which you come to know yourself and the world. Cutting off or deadening your feelings curtails the flow of information to you even more than losing your sense of sight or hearing—either of which would certainly be a devastating loss, but could still be compensated for. There is no other sense that will compensate for the insight and wisdom conferred by your feelings.

All emotions have extremes, with a broad range of intensity. Their arrivals and departures are unpredictable, and they are mostly outside your conscious control. Adults know that although emotions don't necessarily have to be acted upon, it's essential to acknowledge them—to be able to freely own what you feel, even when your emotions make you feel ashamed or vulnerable. As part of your specialized human equipment, emotions must be cared for and understood in the same way in which you care for and try to understand your body. Your health depends on it.

It's essential to come to know your emotions from the inside. They are a vital part of your feedback system with other people and the world around you. They connect you with your history (which determines so much about the day-to-day course of your life) and, in some mystical way we don't really understand, with the unknown. You can come under their sway, get caught in them, and experience them taking charge of your life. But ignoring them doesn't make them go away. It just makes them go underground, where they are truly out of your control.

We can't stress enough that *all* your emotions and feelings have purpose. None of them is without its function. An adult knows and accepts this. Recently, Fran was going to a very important business meeting which had taken a lot of work for her to arrange. "My efforts had centered around pushing through the prohibitions I had about promoting myself. I was halfway over the mountain on my way to the city when I allowed myself to feel the excitement about my success in arranging the meeting. My excitement brought to mind the picture of myself presenting my credentials at the door. At that moment, I realized I had left those credentials on the kitchen table at home. I turned the car around, headed for the documents, and thanked my excitement for saving my day."

Staying Connected

As grownups, we've been trained to lose contact with our interior reality. This creates a formidable barrier to mining our emotions for the riches they hold. If you've been forced to break off contact with your interior, how are you supposed to explore your emotions for information and meaning?

Ordinary emotional responses are distorted in families with grownups as parents, who can neither express nor respond to feelings that make them uncomfortable. For example, childhood fears that are ignored or ridiculed by parents often become a source of chronic anxiety for those children when they grow up. If you find it impossible to relate feelings of anxiety to any rational cause in the present, chances are that they have their roots in the past. Fear, anger, and sadness are a natural part of the array of human emotions and may be firmly anchored in the here and now. Barring a chemical imbalance, chronic anxiety, rage, and depression can develop only over time and are often the result of repressed emotions out of the past. This does nothing to diminish their present power, which for the grownup can be completely overwhelming, coloring every aspect of day-to-day life.

When you know that your identity and worth are safely lodged within you, emotions can become a source of enrichment rather than torture. For example, sadness may be a painful emotion to feel, but when you know that the feeling itself doesn't constitute an emergency, it can help you understand the meaning of a hurt or the magnitude of a loss. Even if an emotion sparks an emergency reaction, you can defuse the emergency by exploring its sources and meaning.

Chronic emotions tell you of something in your psyche that needs attention. They are like radio locator beams from hidden unhealed wounds. They will not go away or stop signaling until you come to the rescue. The more you ignore them, the more power they'll have over you.

All that we say about the internal process of discovering and dealing with repetitive emotions and feelings can also be said about the repetitive thoughts, beliefs, bodily reactions, and fantasies that are out of our conscious control and running our lives. Compulsive thoughts (such as, Maybe I didn't turn off the gas!) can bring some people back to their house countless times, or torment them in the office all day long. A belief that plays itself out incessantly—such as, I am not smart—might color all of someone else's daily interactions. Overpowering exhaustion that automatically surfaces in conflict situations is the same kind of experience interpreted by the body.

The process of becoming conscious of these repetitions, and beginning to see where and how they occur, is the same as that for the emotions. Every person is plagued by internal beasts of one kind or another and is faced with either taming them or being devoured. When Saint-Exupéry's Little Prince asks the fox what taming means, the fox replies, "It means to establish ties . . . One only understands the things that one tames." When the Little Prince asks what he must do to tame the fox, the fox tells him, "You must be very patient. First you will sit down a little distance from me—like that—in the grass. I shall look at you out of the corner of my eye, and you will say nothing. Words are a source of misunderstanding. But you will sit a little closer to me every day." When the Prince has tamed the fox, he says, "I have made him my friend and now he is unique in all the world."

This is good advice for the best way to tame a frightening emotion that keeps repeating itself. Be patient. Pay attention to its message rather than try to rationalize it away. Make friends with it, and let it teach you.

Our friend Caroline runs a very successful catering business. She is a person who hates to feel angry. She admits that anger scares her; but when it arises, which it often does, she controls it by getting busy with other things and finding excuses for other people's bad behavior. At the weekly meetings she held with her staff, her employee who drove the catering truck typically monopolized the time, complaining about various problems with his health and home life and asking for scheduling changes to accommodate his many needs. After every such meeting, Caroline felt angry. One meeting in particular made her so mad that she left when it became clear to her that she wasn't going to be able to control her feelings this time.

Caroline felt horrified with herself for feeling so unsympathetic toward this person, who obviously had so many health problems and whose life seemed like such a complete mess. While sweeping her driveway later that day, she found herself whacking the broom on the lawn over and over again with considerable violence. Part of her stood back in amazement to watch as her anger boiled over. She kept seeing images of her employee in the blades of grass under the broom. In the midst of her fury, she understood the extent to which she'd been manipulated by this man since she'd hired him. The words that came into her head as she was flailing with the broom were *Stop strangling me!*

Caroline was able to connect this with a childhood history of having her progress and self-expression choked off, and feeling obliged as she grew up to continue the process. She saw her driver as just one more person in a long line of people who made her choke off her own needs because theirs were assumed to be more important. At the next meeting, she did not discuss anything about scheduling but demanded to see the books. She discovered numerous errors and, worse, missing entries, which indicated that her driver had pocketed the cash on many occasions. Caroline saw that her fear of anger was costing her money. She saw her working definition of compassion for what it was— a rationalization for her fear of anger. Finally giving her anger a voice changed her way of seeing her life and doing business.

Your personal history colors your every thought and feeling. That's why emotional reactions always have to be examined for any freeloaders from the past. Are you reacting out of the here and now, or has your reaction been distorted by leftover business from the past? To be able to distinguish between the two, you need to know, understand, and acknowledge your personal history.

Of course, this is no easy task—and it's really more a process than a task, as there are always deeper levels of understanding and greater subtleties of insight to be achieved. And your past isn't something that stays fixed, either. With every day you live, your past continues to reveal itself in new ways.

Responses that might have been appropriate for you ten years ago are not necessarily appropriate for you now. You've grown and changed. And yet, when confronted with a situation they found traumatizing in the past, many if not most people will automatically respond in the same way they did then. The same discomfort will come up, the same sense of panic and fear. There will be the same unconsciousness about what's going on. They forget about all the water that's passed under the bridge, and forget about all the choices they can make about how to respond to their feelings. That's why it's so important to be able to sort out the present moment from the past and to give both the past and the present their due. Your emotional capacities can bloom and thrive when you know and appreciate the history of your heart.

Adults actively seek a greater understanding of their personal past, knowing its value to their freedom of choice in the present. If you're stuck in frustrating or destructive emotional patterns, it's usually because something from your past is blocking your ability to learn from your emotions and continue to grow. If every time a shaming or painful thought, conversation, or feeling comes up you have to run away from it, your life is going to be an experience of averting your eyes, not hearing, missing the point, and failing to notice what's happening right under your nose. Your parents' emotional handicaps will resurface in one form or another to become your handicaps, and then your children's. If you don't spot these problems now and begin to learn about them, the cycle will just continue. As Harriet Goldhor Lerner notes in *The Dance of Intimacy*, "We all have important emotional issues and if we don't process them up the generations, we are more than likely to pass them down."

Emotions that plague you with their continual reappearances in your life are actually gold mines to be explored, for they contain information about who and what you are. When you're willing to look at them and claim them—to tame them, in Saint-Exupéry's words—you greatly expand your options. A friend told us recently, "There is nothing more satisfying than to see an emotion that once

127

plagued me come up, to recognize it for what it is, understand the information it's giving me, and then watch it recede without claiming my attention for hours and hours all day long."

Making Room in Your Life for Emotional Complexity

As adults, we have a dual responsibility to be clear about our own motivation in expressing or not expressing an emotion, while at the same time being concerned with the effect of our choices on others. It's often assumed that being peaceful gives rise only to peacefulness. However, there are many adults abused as children who will tell you that one parent's need for peace allowed another parent's abuse to continue. Was that peacefulness or just numbing? Having a clear understanding of your emotions and their effects on yourself and others is as important as any of your other survival skills. And yet there are no courses in school with anger, sadness, or love on the curriculum, and you don't earn merit badges for owning your feelings as a Boy Scout or a Brownie.

It's important to accept the fact that we don't know all there is to know about our emotions and their effects, both on ourselves and on others. To some extent, the unconscious is always part of the loop. We do things we think are benignly motivated for the good of another, and are rudely awakened to the hurt and resentment those actions have in reality caused. Becoming aware of the complexity woven through our emotional life is an adult task.

This was illustrated by a friend of ours who lives in a small town and is involved with the community of recovering alcoholics. Our friend was considering whether she wanted to begin working with a local therapist. "But everyone knows everyone's business here," she told us, "and what you don't know, you can hear at the local diner." This lack of privacy made her feel vulnerable. She felt awfully uncomfortable about the idea that the whole community would know that she'd chosen to go into therapy, and she even felt a little distrustful of the therapist's ability to keep her secrets safe, just by virtue of where he lived and worked. Despite her intense discomfort, she kept repeating an AA slogan to herself: You are only as sick as your secrets.

Whatever wisdom there may be in this statement, it wasn't necessarily the right adage to be following in this particular situation. The grownup was in charge of our friend's decision to see a therapist. As grownups will, she was trying to "get it right." She used the AA slogan as a way of talking herself out of her healthy reluctance to be a topic of group conversation. We assured her that she had a right to take her feelings of vulnerability and her need for privacy seriously. They constituted a first step toward intimacy with herself. Later, after reflection, she decided to see a therapist outside her community.

Glossing over feelings may promote conformity, but it works against your sense of trust in yourself. Grownups buy into belief systems and then rigidly apply their principles. Just saying everything you can think of to say about yourself in public doesn't produce intimacy with oneself or with others. Protecting the secret life of the soul is not the same as protecting the secrets of a dysfunctional family. Healthy adults know the difference and have enough self-esteem to honor their own needs for privacy.

A workaholic client gave Lou a description of the devastating emotional confusion in which old and new emotions are hopelessly mixed, even in someone with a high degree of inner awareness. "When I stop working, I immediately feel useless—as if I don't contribute to life. The thought that I don't deserve to be here surfaces, and then panic sets in. I try to control these thoughts and emotions, but they come anyway in a devastating spiral. Who can tell me that I'm all right, that I don't have to prove myself all the time? Rationally, I know I'm all right. But what do I do about the body sensations that completely undermine any rational sense of well-being? I get classic panic symptoms: confused thinking, sweaty palms, racing heart, vertigo. My own voice suddenly has no authority. An argument rages back and forth in my mind, but the panicked part of me always seems like it's going to win—so I have to fight even harder to keep it under control. It's so exhausting that work always seems like a restful alternative."

The next time you feel a feared emotion rising, take an adult stance and say to yourself: Okay, here it comes. I hate it, but I know it won't kill me. I don't have to respond now. I can take as much time as I need to figure out what's going on. If someone demands an immediate response, I can say, "I can't answer that right now, but I'll get back to you."

Take a few moments to contemplate the information you gather about the occasion that sparked the emotion. Are there similarities to the last time, and the time before that? What are they, and what do they say about your relationship to that particular set of circumstances, that particular person?

Obsessive patterns of anxiety, depression, and anger can be interrupted in two basic ways. First, you can practice recognizing the pattern and describing it. One client of Lou's calls his patterns "sad kid toys." Another, who had trouble with chronic anger, describes it this way: "Way before I'm really angry, I get all kinds of other signals, like confusion: I can't understand what someone is saying to me, or what I'm supposed to be doing. Another signal is when I'm convinced that what I'm doing has

—
130

no value—it's just no good, whatever I've done or made. If people appreciate whatever it is, or praise me, they must be lying. It takes letting those signals in for a while before I get the message about being angry. And listening slows me down enough so I can really think about the situation and what other things might be going on."

The second thing you can do when caught in a swirl of emotion is to remind yourself that there are no emergencies. Tell yourself to take a deep breath. You have time to consider the situation and the way you're feeling. Remember that you're feeling a complex of emotions from the past. Some of them are relevant to your present situation, and some of them aren't. But now is not the time to take directives from any of them. The state you're in has compromised your ability to hear correctly, much less act correctly.

The state of emotional upheaval, and whatever degree of adult thinking you can conjure up inside you, can coexist until the wounded grownup part of you gives up ground little by little. It *will* eventually recede, because your adult has not rejected or judged the grownup voices inside you, but accepted them. As you get better at this, you can even allow a feeling of love to well up and enfold the one inside who has suffered the emotional consequences of early wounding. The difficult moment passes.

Ultimately, the adult must take the position of an intimate witness to emotion and feeling. Adults feel what they're feeling, but they're also consciously aware of the complexity of emotion and the wealth of information it has to offer. Even if they get carried away by what they're feeling, they reserve a small part of themselves to watch the passage. They become like writers: Everything they see and feel has value as well as a multiplicity of meaning. Everything, pleasant and unpleasant, is grist for their mill.

In the "I" of the Storm

Try this exercise after you've been in a storm of emotions but before you react by doing anything. Close your eyes. Take three deep breaths, letting each breath fill your belly, and then empty your belly. Make sure your attention is placed fully on the sensations of your belly rising and falling. Notice that you are now in contact with the sensations in your belly, as well as witnessing those sensations: Your inner "I" is the witness. Now have your inner "I" recall the emotions contained in the storm. Watch the emotions, and the emotions spawning more emotions, swirling around. As they dance by, name them, or let them have an image: There is my anger rising up in my body like a flame. There is my frustration at that person's obviousness. There is the joy I feel at seeing my child; there is my fear as I watch him crossing the street. There is my fear about my fear. There are my judgments about being angry.

Notice that your inner "I" is separate from this experience, watching without judgment. If you lose contact with the inner "I," take your attention away from the emotions and return to deep breathing for three more rounds. Then go back to watching your emotions. The witnessing adult state wants us to have understanding, peacefulness, and healing, and will guide us through our emotional storms at a pace we can tolerate.

CHAPTER SEVEN

I Know There Is Nothing But Now

*"We make a journey to the "promised land" . . .
and we have arrived when we realize that we were
there all along."*

—Chogyam Trungpa

One of the characteristics of authentic adults is that they are present in the moment, whether that moment is painful or pleasurable. This is possible because adults can accept whatever is so in the moment without trying to change it, no matter how they feel about it, or what reactions are evoked. As explained in the previous chapter, the ability of adults to be open to their internal experience, acknowledge its existence, and value what it has to tell them is in stark contrast to grownup behavior. Grownups have been trained to ignore their insides and stick exclusively to "reality." This makes the grownup's experience of the moment glancing, constricted, and relatively superficial compared to what's possible for the adult. The grownup's operating principle in this regard is *I must manage the moment and not let it surprise me.* The adult's, on the other hand, is *I know there is nothing but now.*

For many people in our modern world, it feels as though there's always too much to do at any given moment. This makes it hard to savor and focus on the present with your full conscious awareness. When you have "down time," you may be too physically and emotionally exhausted to experience it fully. Most people have a largely unfocused, distracted, and constricted experience of the present. Their fully experienced moments, when they are totally absorbed, are rare and valuable. These are the peak experiences you have in sports and love, the moments of spontaneous creation, the flash of a great idea, the epiphanies of understanding, the intuition that lets you know exactly what you have to do, the times when you are in nature and feel yourself as part of the whole, the moments with loved ones when your heart rests easy, the simple times when you are connected and you know it. Think how rich life would be if all your moments were like this.

In his book *The Evolving Self,* Mihaly Csikszentmihalyi talks about what he calls being in the experience of "flow," which involves an absorption in the moment and a release of profound abilities. He says that one of the most often mentioned features of this experience is "the sense of discovery, the excitement of finding out something new about oneself, or about the possibilities of interacting with the many opportunities for action that the environment offers." When you have to manage the moment and not let it surprise you, this kind of experience becomes impossible.

Most North Americans and many other people in the developed world spend their lives in a frenzy of pursuit or flight, telling themselves now and then that they will stop soon and begin to enjoy the luxuries or financial security or professional success or the dream of finally getting organized they've worked so hard to attain. For grownups, the possibility of fulfillment and pleasure almost always lies in the future. And even then, it's highly conditional and managed. In the saddest cases, it has been given up on entirely for a life lived in a state of deadness and dullness, where even the pursuit of happiness has been forgotten.

Fran recalls: "I will never forget the moment when I knew I hadn't consciously been in the moment for years. I was at work at the end of a hot summer afternoon. The whole team was sitting around, tired after completing a project. I made one last suggestion about a possible improvement. 'This is it, Fran,' one of my colleagues told me dismissively. When I went back to my desk, I saw that indeed this was it for this project—all my hopes for somehow making it better were futile.

"Thinking about it further, I saw that I was living my life the way I had been living the project—focused on the future, where things would be different from the way they were now. It's not bad per se to live this way, it's just a loss of the rich experience of living in the here and now. I saw that I didn't think of myself as Fran as she was in the present moment, but as the person I was going to be when I had fixed myself up, when everything would be as I felt it should be. I really didn't live in the small apartment I hated, but in the house I was going to own one day My job was just temporary until I could get my real career started. I saw there was nothing about the moment that I liked, so I didn't live there.

"I realized that I had to start paying attention in the moment to each of these aspects of my life, making changes. It wasn't easy, because below each obvious problem—a job I hated, an apartment I hated, a self I hated—were layers of emotional, mental, and habitual conditioning which denied me permission to be fully present in my own life."

What does *being in the moment* mean? Bear with us, because dissecting these concepts in writing is rather tricky. First, am I conscious at all of the fact that I—as a distinct entity, safe and sound inside my own skin—am in a moment? To be conscious that I'm in a moment means that I must have some sense of an internal self, an "I" who is an intimate witness both to who I am and what is happening just now. For grownups trained to ignore their inner life, the sense of an "I" who observes and knows is unavailable. The grownup has some superficial data about this "self," but no direct experience of it.

Second, how fully conscious am I in a given moment? Our capacity for richness and depth of experience in any given moment is virtually limitless. But awareness of the moment has both pleasant and unpleasant components. Becoming fully aware may mean understanding how much you don't want to be in the moment, or how constricted your awareness feels in the moment, or to what degree you are in an emergency state in the moment. Being in the here and now doesn't always mean experiencing a wonderful expansion of consciousness. It can and often does mean that in addition to being more conscious of what is comfortable, fulfilling, and joyous for you, you're expanding your awareness to include stuff that feels awful, that you absolutely hate, and would like to disown completely. You can't have one without being open to the other. So you can't be fully in the moment, even for your joy, if you're editing out the sadness or pain.

Loss of the Present Moment and the Grownup's Sense of Emptiness

Being fully present in the moment requires many moments of hard work, hammering away at your raw material until suddenly you have a jewel. There are lots of reasons why you may not be consciously present in your own moment, sometimes for hours, days, and years at a time. People are raised to be permanently entranced by the version of reality presented to them by their parents, teachers, family stories, religions, and so on. They skim through life on automatic pilot, unaware that they're not in contact with the reality within and around them. Their experiences often seem meaningless and superficial; they don't know why they feel so empty. They rarely break free of this trance to allow themselves to see everything with new eyes. Almost dying seems to do the trick sometimes. But we believe that you should be able to be fully alive in the moment without having to go through the trauma of a dire illness or a near-death experience.

How is it that we lose what we see so often in young children—that absorption in the moment so complete that they don't even hear their parents talking to them from a couple of feet away? We recently saw a scene in a supermarket that gave us a clue. A toddler was wailing because he had run down the aisle, tripped, and fallen. His cries were his response to his bruised knee and the sense of unfairness and embarrassment that come with an unexpected fall. He was probably also upset with being on the shopping expedition in the first place, and his harried-looking mother wasn't doing anything to make it more pleasant or interesting for him. Seeming to be at the end of her rope, she said to him harshly, "I'll give you something real to cry about if you don't stop that noise." She didn't offer him any comfort or any understanding.

It's not hard to imagine a voice somewhere in that child's head telling him, "Get out, get out of here, run from this if you know what's good for you. This hurt and this crying are dangerous. Run to something else. Anything will do. Run from this moment, make it not real." Gershen Kaufman in his book *Shame* talks about the "blaming parent" who needs to find reasons for things that go wrong. Often the child is the most convenient scapegoat. "A part of the child then identifies with the parent and begins to treat himself with contempt."

Self-hatred is not something we are born with. It is acquired layer by layer over a period of time. We get chased out of our experience, and bullied into "growing up" and managing our moments to prevent surprise and spare our parents their own moments of painful awareness. This story is repeated over and over again in our lives as we encounter parents, teachers, and role models who can't tolerate our moments, because they remind them of moments that they themselves were forced to give up. We learn to hate the parts of ourselves that cause us so much trouble with caregivers, and so we move away from them as effectively as we can.

For well-trained grownups, many thoughts, sensations, memories, and associations have to be censored from their experience of any given moment because of the possibility of being thrown into a psychic emergency. Much of our energy is engaged in editing out those parts of each moment that are unacceptable or threatening for whatever reason. This leaves us little energy left over to be fully in the moment, experience it thoroughly, and see what it holds. In the process of protecting ourselves, we lose our experience.

People forced in childhood to edit out the internal "I" that might have made contact with their moments can end up lying on their deathbeds, wondering who they are and where their life went. A minister friend of ours told us his experience of this. He went to the hospital to visit two members of his church, who were both dying of cancer. The first woman he visited complained bitterly about her lot in life, asking piteously, "Why me?" She complained about her relatives and friends, saying that they weren't doing enough for her, and noting that that's how they always were, so why should she be surprised? Our friend gave what comfort he could, and then went to visit the other dying woman, who greeted him with enthusiasm. "Come in," she said.

"You're just the person I want to see. You know I am dying, and I have work to do. I want your help. I've had a full and wonderful life, and I want to gather up the fruits of it before I go. This is my last adventure. I don't know if there will be adventures after death, but I hope so. I like adventures."

There was little difference in the medical situation each of these women found herself in. And yet one continued to miss the richness of her present moments, and the other squeezed her last moments for whatever adventure they held. She was ready to open her eyes to see, and open her heart to experience, whatever life—even in death—had in store for her.

Each of these women is doing the best she can with what she is conscious of in the moment. We tell these stories because they illustrate the choice you have in the way you experience the moments of your life right up to the moment of your death. Each moment contains the potential for the experience of fullness and satisfaction, even in the worst of circumstances. If you have a sense of the internal "I" that is uniquely and inviolably you, you can choose to be present and take what is offered by all the moments that make up your life.

The Disappearing Act

In fact, you are always in the moment—only your personal awareness of it changes. The moment is always there in its fullness and factuality. It is you who are absent. Arthur Deikman says in his book *The Observing Self,* "Unlike every other aspect of experience—thoughts, emotions, desires, and functions—the observing self can be known but not located, not 'seen.'"

Awareness is such a primary reality that we cannot examine it, we can only experience it. As an example, close your eyes and let yourself be aware of your body. Now bring your awareness to some part of your body that is outside your awareness, and feel it—for example, your little toe or the back of your wrist. When you do this, what happens? Something that was there all along suddenly enters your awareness. Somehow you were able to bring your awareness to this "thing" and touch it directly with your consciousness. This awareness is part of the famous koan, If a tree falls in the forest, and no one is present, does it make a sound?

So you thought about bringing your awareness to your toe or the back of your wrist, and then you did it. Doing it was not the same as thinking it. Your toe did not change by having your attention on it. *Attention* is just another word for the awareness that you—your internal "I"—brought to it.

Crucial to the example is that you did it consciously. You consciously used consciousness. Animal consciousness shifts, but the shifts are unconscious, driven by pain and pleasure (for example, a thorn in the toe). Animals are fully in the moment in terms of content. They are capable of experiencing the fullness that their sensory equipment will allow. But they are not conscious either that it is *a* moment or that it is *their* moment. The awareness of awareness is uniquely human and uniquely adult. This capacity is integral to the internal "I" described in chapter 3.

We measure our moments as time. The experience of time is essentially different for the adult and the grownup. The adult experiences time as an infinitely flexible container. Adults have all the time they need, and they sense its fullness. It can be moving fast or slowly, but there is no shortage of it.

Grownups experience time in a couple of different but related ways. One way is as a closing door they have to squeeze through. The door is closing too fast for everything the grownup wants to include. Fitting everything in becomes an emergency situation. This concept of time is goal-oriented and linear. There's no time to make any one particular moment special. Every moment is, in a sense, lost before it's ever experienced.

The grownup's other concept of time is as a featureless plain interrupted only by dramatic events such as death or illness. The grownup's need to deny interior reality creates tunnel vision and a narrow focus for all his faculties as they hone in either on a solution to a never-ending crisis state, or the quickest path to numbness and relief. He is like a lifeguard at the beach on a day when the surf is high and dangerous. If you were to ask the lifeguard about the smell and color of the sea, he probably couldn't tell you anything about it, because all his senses are focused on averting disaster. Any broader sense of perspective is lost; anything that can't contribute to a solution becomes irrelevant. This type of emergency prevention response is a state of being for the grownup.

When we cannot be in the moment, we are frozen—stuck in the past or trying to control the future. It becomes impossible to accurately assess either the safety or the danger of our present situation. We cannot creatively move with change—change simply carries us along. At junctures where we might make a change easier or more to our liking, we're not present in a way that would allow us to seize the moment of opportunity. Instead we're focused on a controlling timetable, or a goal that remains forever out of reach. Having goals is not the cause of this experience of insufficiency. It's the unconscious panic that we are not all right which drives the striving. People who live in this state all the time lose a lot. There is a difference between a deliberately focused attention in the moment, and compulsively narrow awareness driven by the need to keep fear or pain unconscious.

Spaced out, airhead, flaky, the lights are on, but nobody's home—all these phrases evoke the absence of a person's conscious awareness in a given moment. Such behaviors—forgetting something important because you're so preoccupied, being unable to respond appropriately to what someone has said because you haven't been listening, remaining in situations that are physically harmful—are actually learned responses. They protected us in prior circumstances when the only way of managing a terrifying situation was to diminish our consciousness of it.

There are many ways in which grownups disappear from the here and now: living isolated in a stream of uncommunicated thoughts or sensations, living in the past or the future, refusing to deal with the daily routines of life, projecting false stupidity or incompetence, being a know-it-all, ignoring the body altogether or losing touch with a particular part of it, being addicted, falling asleep at crucial moments, or never completing a thought, a conversation, or a project. A client told Lou, "For years I walked on my heels until one day a gym coach pointed out that my toes looked like they wished they were somewhere else. I never made complete contact with the ground when I walked. I couldn't allow the conscious thought, but my feet weren't shy about saying the truth about not wanting to be on this earth."

Each family passes down its own unique version of life's dangers—and we're not referring to the universal dangers posed by fire, hurricanes, or running in front of cars. In both of our families, for example, there were dire consequences if adults suspected that you saw their shame or doubt about anything. In many families, fear is so dangerous that it can be communicated only as rage; sadness and loss are so feared that they can only be drowned in alcohol. Other families can't tolerate anyone knowing about their finances, or the skeletons in their closet. If you happen to see these things as a child, you become a trespasser in peril of dire consequences (usually, a total withdrawal of parental affection or some other form of emotional anathema). You have to hide the part of you that has borne witness to what was supposed to remain hidden, perhaps even denying your own memory of what you saw. A major piece of the grownup facade we put together is the increasing ability to hide and not even remember where parts of the self are buried. Not seeing these things becomes habitual even after we have left our families of origin and have families of our own.

There is a lot of acceptance for disappearing in our culture. "Oh, she's just spaced out," people say—as if that really explains anything. Most of us don't want to know what's behind our own and other people's closed doors. For grownups taught to dismiss their internal experience, there is little desire to understand the events that prompt disappearing from the moment, sometimes for hours at a time. We heard an adult child of alcoholics say, "When I smell booze on anyone's breath, I want to run—and sometimes I do, finding myself only hours later, wondering how so much time passed without my even noticing." Identifying the triggers that launch your own disappearing acts are the first step toward learning to be more present in the moment. This can happen only through understanding and owning your history, and becoming aware of the shaming forces and unspoken rules that prevailed in your family and community while you were growing up.

Grownups don't question their behaviors, ideas, goals, or the attitudes they were taught by their parents, teachers, and community. They don't see why they should, and they wouldn't know how to go about it if they did, because they've been taught so well to ignore the importance of family patterns and repetitive behavior. They've completely bought in to the idea that the past has no relevance. By their lights, the damaging consequences of their words and actions have no echo in their personal history; and yet they live wrapped up in that history like a larva wrapped in a cocoon, insulated from both the pleasures and pain of the present moment.

Adults, on the other hand, have learned to look at their present patterns of behavior and question whether they may be ineffective coping mechanisms left over from the past. They want to see the motivations and expectations that may be coloring their lives now, especially if these are undermining their opportunities to make choices. This isn't a morbid interest in the past, but a form of commitment to the present: Adults want their present moments to be as unencumbered as possible, to have all five senses in full operating order. They want to experience every present moment to the fullest extent possible.

An ongoing intimate relationship with your inner experience produces a fuller sense of yourself in each moment, even though at some of those moments the grownup in you will be in charge. This is not something to beat yourself up over. The ongoing process is rather one of letting go; and letting go of old behaviors, assumptions, patterns, fears, and hopes doesn't happen immediately, because we have many ways of hanging on to the strategies we credit with saving us. One of the first assumptions adults let go of is that the grownup part of themselves will miraculously disappear and never trouble them again. Our defenses have a life of their own and don't necessarily know that times have changed. Dropping them means that you've begun to see them, catch them in the act, and accept them. The trick is to acknowledge them for the job they did, which is no longer needed, and at the same time acknowledge your desire for a more expanded life for yourself—which does not include your outdated coping mechanisms from the past. It's a moment-by-moment process of acceptance and change, and it takes time.

Getting Beyond Your Image

Almost all your emotional education has been in the preparation and maintenance of the image or facade you present to yourself and the world. The more you are identified with your image, the less you will have a separate sense of an "I" to which you can refer when you want to create an independent standpoint. Perhaps your facade has one primary defining statement: I am a mother . . . I am fat . . . I am gentle and kind . . . I always screw up . . . I am accomplished . . . I always tell the truth . . . I am attractive. In such ways, your sense of "I" is never separated from functions or characteristics. You find your only meaning in being a mother, even after your children are grown. Or you stick to your rule of being gentle and kind and not getting angry, even in situations in which you're clearly being exploited. Or you find it devastating as you grow older to find that people aren't responding to your looks the way they used to. Some people make the same exclusive identification of themselves as "wounded." But we are much more than the sum total of our wounds. Any label that has to remain true all the time will inevitably rob you of part of your experience and part of your life.

Reflection and contemplation of the things that happen from day to day are methods for coming into contact with that "I" space inside, getting the feel of it, and beginning to recognize it from moment to moment. You can practice this. At the end of a day, take an experience that was mildly disturbing for you and replay it. Then replay it again, but this time stand aside and comment on it as if you were watching it as a sporting event. Notice the difference between the two types of reporting. Which one gave you a sense that you could expand your choices about who you are? There are many excellent books on this subject, some of which are listed in the bibliography. We would especially recommend Deikman's *The Observing Self: Mysticism and Psychotherapy* and Kabat-Zinn's *Wherever You Go, There You Are: Mindfulness Meditation in Everyday Life.*

Everyone has had those periods of tortured insomnia when you play an unpleasant event over and over in your head, replaying what was said and obsessing about what should have been said. It is a fruitless and unsatisfying experience, and very different from viewing the same event from the vantage point of the inner observer. This is the essential difference between grownup controlling and adult reflection. When you look at difficult memories from the adult point of view, you're not simply reliving the experience and you're not trying to make it different. Rather, you're accepting it as it occurred and using it as a learning tool, knowing that who you are is separate from your problems and pains or the outcome of a particular situation. You're therefore not forced into justifications, rationalizations, and excuses (or any other emergency prevention response), which would further mire you in the past and yank you out of the present moment.

The experience of internal reflection is often described as "relaxing down" to another level of awareness, looking at larger interactions rather than focusing on specific exchanges. For example, in thinking about my habitually unpleasant exchanges with Mabel, I notice that I always feel like she's trying to put me down. Shifting to a larger focus, I can see that I've made an assumption about Mabel's intentions that's not necessarily true. When I respond to Mabel by saying something hurtful in return,

I'm acting on that possibly false assumption. Knowing that I've probably hurt Mabel is unpleasant knowledge that I'd like to shut out of my awareness—this becomes clear to me. It's also clear how I immediately come up with a rationale about how she deserves her comeuppance anyway; and I say something even more offensive and hurtful. I notice that my offensiveness is defensive and ask myself what is it that I feel so defensive about. What is impelling this robotlike round of reactions? Giving it some thought, I can remember some of the people who taught me that I was not okay, and I think about why I still believe them. Then I tell myself that I am basically okay, factually okay, even if there are some things I still can't accept about myself. I can decide that I would prefer not to complicate an already complicated interior situation by dragging Mabel into it.

That's one way the interior process of learning from your problems and letting them go might play itself out when you can use the adult sense of an "I" to guide your exploration.

The experience of the moment is varied and changeable. There is no "right" content to a conscious moment; and most moments have a tremendous amount of content. Our freedom is not in what is given in them, but in how we move with what is given. Often, when we lose consciousness that "I am here now," and then return to awareness, the first thing that our awareness touches on is the reason we left. This moment of returning to awareness—even when it's unpleasant—can be a gateway to a deeper and richer conscious contact with your experience of your innermost self.

Lou remembers when he was sitting in a board of directors meeting with an unexplained sense of anxiety gnawing at the pit of his stomach. "The board of a community organization was meeting to review a hostile response the organization had received from a powerful local political group. There was a lot of emotion in the room, with a lot of defensiveness for 'our' side and criticism of 'their' side. At one point, I noticed how shallow my breathing was and I took a deep breath. With that breath of awareness, I was back in my own skin again, feeling the fear of conflict that was in my stomach. Because I was able to stay with that feeling, I realized that the fear was an old one left over from childhood, of being attacked by my older brother and various bullies in my life. The realization put my present fear in perspective—I was no longer a vulnerable, gawky adolescent. I relaxed and breathed easier and was able to pass on my own feelings of reassurance to the other members of the board. 'This isn't an emergency,' I told them. 'I think what we need to do is just keep on doing what we feel is useful for the community and maintain a dialogue with the people who oppose us.' The discussion was able to move on in a more confident mode in which we were able to face our problems and decide on a course of action."

There are two different ways of being "lost in the moment." One way is filling, the other is draining. These ways are more easily recognizable by their byproducts than by the moments themselves. Being deeply conscious and absorbed in the moment (one version of being lost in the moment) leaves you feeling enriched, nourished, satisfied, and alive. You could be sitting at the shoreline, watching the waves; lying in a hammock, looking at the pattern of leaves against the sky; doing dishes, totally lost in a fantasy; becoming completely absorbed in a book or a film; or losing yourself in the throes of passion or creative expression. What you're doing is not as important as the quality of your presence in the activity. "Coming to" from the other kind of lost-in-the-moment feeling—from having *not* been present—leaves you empty, vacant, and lost. In the former, there is an expansion of personal experience; in the latter, a diminishment. But even the second kind, as demonstrated by Lou's story, holds opportunities for increasing your personal awareness. Remaining in that uncomfortable space, and being with yourself through it to the next moment, is the way an adult stays present and taps into the rich sources of information and ability deeper within.

Adults know that they are not in control of the world, nor of most of what happens in it. They also know that nothing is permanent. Things, people, places, organizations—all of these change. The adult doesn't waste any time trying to manipulate the past into staying as is. That's a full-time job for most grownups.

The Intimacy of Life in the Present Moment

Pleasant changes aren't usually a problem for any of us. Getting a better job, or making more money, or falling in love, or having a child are the stuff of big changes in life—and they have their difficulties—but such changes are usually welcome. It is the unpleasant changes that cause us so much trouble. It causes problems right away if we try to stop an unwanted change. As the cliché goes, there are only two things we can be sure of: death and taxes. And yet, even beyond death and taxes, the moment— and our awareness of it—is the only certainty we can count on to be constantly available. Finding systems and tools to develop the moment and our awareness of it is the job of the adult. Everything else is subject to change without notice.

A woman we work with told us her experience of a co-worker who had cancer. The woman was so adamant about getting better that she refused to even talk about her illness. "The C-word" was verboten in her office, and everyone was supposed to go along with the pretense that Karen was fine. They were prevented from giving their sympathy, help, and comfort to their friend and colleague who was suffering in front of them. Keeping up the subterfuge was completely alienating. People who had been close to Karen drew away from her. She was so frozen in time, and fighting so hard to keep change out of her life, that she missed all the support that the people around her were longing to give. Her energy was spent on denial, with little left over for healing or comfort, and she died without ever acknowledging her own reality. It was a miserable experience for everyone involved. When we live in the past or the future, we lose touch with intimacy, emotions, power, intuition, and the senses. Dying in such a state, we lose our life twice over.

It's easy to say, "Stay in the moment." It's another thing to actually stay there when you are trembling with doubt, fear, or pain like the woman who had cancer. If we are lucky, someone may stand beside us at those times, and that can help. But the hard part is to stay in our own skin while the fire of pain and fear rages inside. Why bother to make that effort? Because the moment is the conscious access point for everything. It is the gateway to our lives. From a practical point of view, any other starting point is going to lead to inaccuracy and, eventually, we are going to have to work our way back to that spot anyway. Those moments we run from keep circling us and swooping relentlessly until we stand to face them.

It's a curious paradox in this life that change is a constant, dependable, and unchanging fact. But when we try to control the moment by denying what is so, we have lost the moment to the past or the future. Trying to alter the moment steals it from us. If we want fruitful change in our lives, we have to move through each moment, experiencing its wholeness, savoring what it has to offer, noticing where we are stuck, and in the process maintain an intimate contact with our deepest sense of self. A poem by the thirteenth-century Sufi poet Rumi captures the spirit of this effort:

Today like every other day
We wake up empty and scared.
Don't open the door of your study and begin reading.
Take down a musical instrument.
Let the beauty we live be what we do.
There are hundreds of ways to kneel and kiss the earth.

It is not only for the experience of change that we need to be conscious in the moment, but for the experience of intimacy as well. Being conscious in the moment automatically confers a kind of intimacy with whatever our awareness is touching at that moment, be it something in nature, a line of thoughtful exploration, something we fear, an unhappy aspect of our own insides, another person's story, another person's body, or any combination thereof. The adult is comfortable with this intimacy. The grownup, on the other hand, is characterized by the inability to make contact, or, at best, by a need to control contact. This avoidance of intimacy is accomplished in any number of ordinary ways: talking too fast or talking nonstop, interrupting, not listening, making points rather than responding, staying only on the intellectual or technical plane ("talking shop"), never talking about your own feelings or personal history, and so on.

The need for closeness and intimacy never goes away. Even the grownup who fears it feels the void and tries to fill it—perhaps through food, drugs, alcohol, romance, fanaticism, or other forms of escapism. The experience of intimacy—with our bodies, emotions, or thought processes; with another; with nature;

—
153

with the unknown; with the creative process; with community; with our ancestors—is nourishment for our hearts and souls. Without this nourishment, our hearts and souls wither.

Some people feel that one of the scariest things in life is to look directly into another person's eyes in silence. The intimacy of this—the exposure—feels too great to bear. Such people are in deadly fear of having their flaws—or the other person's flaws—brought to light. For this same reason, they may find it unbearable to look for a long time into their own eyes in a mirror.

To look into the eyes of someone who is in pain or dying can be even harder. Adults know that they can be with themselves and others even in moments of pain. They can influence the material conditions surrounding someone's pain to support that person's movement *through* it: They can give food, clothing, shelter, and care. They can listen; they can give of their own empathy and understanding. They can give of themselves.

Intimacy is what satisfies us, although most of us don't act as though we believe that, and we rarely do the work necessary to achieve it. To want and seek intimate contact comes naturally to adults, who know that they must stay with each aspect of their being as it presents itself in the moment. What comes into each of our moments asks us to be with it. The experiences range from the sublime to the ridiculous and everything in between.

Whether you are in your grownup or your adult mode, or some combination of both, the moment is the container for the intangible experiences that make you feel and act like a human being. Love is an outgrowth of intimacy. To consciously connect with yourself and then with another human being is one of the most satisfying experiences in life. We see, we are seen. We touch, we are touched. The open wounds of the grownup have an opportunity to close and heal.

This intimacy and healing also occur when we step out into our community and truly open our eyes and hearts to what is there. Intimacy is about being, not doing—although enlightened doing flows from it. When we really see what is there on our city streets, in the faces of children, in our families, and in images of people around the world, we are clearing the pathway toward giving whatever strength and help we have to offer, whatever love, whatever shared moments in the here and now.

Eye to "I"

The more times you can simply be in the moment with yourself, the more times you will be able to be in the moment in general. Here's an exercise you can do every day. At the end of the day, or when you go into the bathroom before you leave work, or to wash your hands before dinner, or at bedtime, take five minutes to be with yourself in the mirror. Stand quietly in front of the mirror and look yourself in the eye. Keep conscious contact with yourself. Really look at yourself. What do you feel? What comes up that makes you look away? Is this similar to anything that comes up between you and someone else? How difficult is it to keep looking at yourself for more than a minute? Does being unable to be with the person closest to you make you sad? Do this exercise every day for a week, noticing your reactions and feelings about it. Is there a difference at the end of the week in the quality of your time with yourself? Don't evaluate this in terms of good or bad performance. This is a relationship you are forging, not a morality play.

CHAPTER EIGHT

I Always Have Power

*"Power is a living, mutable force that exists amongst us;
it is as palpable as our breath, a tender look, a word of love
or shout of anger."*

– John Wood

Personal power lies within each of us. The passage to conscious adulthood necessitates coming to know that power and owning and experiencing it fully.

Most people talk about power as an external phenomenon involving status, domination, and winning. Personal power and personal aggressiveness are often confused. When someone in the news is described as powerful, most often what comes to people's minds are such things as position, possessions, or the number of countries or people under this person's sway. In the United States, the notion of power is much more closely identified with force or dominance than with ability and the fulfillment of potential. Power is not seen as a process, but a fait accompli.

What the adult knows is that power is inherent in every person. It does not reside in position nor in the use of particular tools or weapons, although it can at times make use of them. Rather, personal power resides in your conscious internal contact with your inherent abilities, and the expansion and deepening of that contact as you exercise your power. You are an intimate, internal witness to your body moving, your mind as it follows a train of thought, your creativity as it transforms what is into what might be, and your emotions as they touch you. This experience of witnessing enables you as an adult to come to know your powers better, to experience ownership of them, and to have a joyful and grateful sense of responsibility for them. Adults know that they own their powers, but are also deeply aware of them as givens, as gifts.

The adult also knows that personal power is inherently limited. None of us is omnipotent or all-powerful. Unless we knowingly accept this state of affairs, the unrealistic, grandiose demands we make on ourselves thwart our ability to learn and be creative and deny us the knowledge of our personal power that is basically our due.

This is where the grownup runs into problems. All but the most sociopathic grownups would tell you that they know they have limits. The difficulty is that, on an unconscious level, most people harbor a different and conflicting set of beliefs about how their power *should* be unlimited. These underlying beliefs cause grownups to respond to their limits as if they were flaws. Because limits are seen as flaws, the grownup feels compelled to hide them. Grownups trained to deny internal experience may, in fact, have the use of many of their powers, but are not conscious of them as such; they cannot intimately witness them. Unlike adults, grownups do not experience ownership of their powers, nor do they have as much freedom to choose which ones to call on, or when or how to use them. The grownup is largely reactive. He may use his powers well, but does not possess them in the sense that a master carpenter possesses his tools. He does not have an internal "I" to possess them with. The grownup's powers are not part of the picture he has of himself. He has learned to focus outside himself on measurable results, and experiences his power only in terms of results. His internal process is neither valued nor seen for what it is—as the ground from which all his powers spring to life.

In this chapter, we'll talk about power. The following chapter addresses the question of limits. Bear in mind, though, that the two really go hand-in-hand.

The Adult's Power Bank

Your basic powers arise from:

• Your body, which has the power of movement, grasping and releasing, balancing, and the five senses.

• Your intellect, with the power to reflect, remember, and fantasize; analyze the information gathered by your senses; and create and comprehend language.

• Your imagination, which enables you to express your own vision of the world or your innermost feelings in words, sound, visual images, and movement.

• Your creativity, which allows you to play, invent, imagine, destroy, and rebuild.

• Your intuition, which enables you to know other human beings intimately, to grasp the nonrational, and to apprehend the unknown.

• Your emotions, which allow you to experience and directly respond to your inner life, other people, and the world, without language or analysis.

• Your will, which conveys the power to make choices, take action, persist, and let go.

This is by no means an exhaustive compendium, and most of these elements are usually absent from any discussion of personal power. The point of listing them is to put our consciousness back on them, because most of the time these powers are taken for granted. The ability to learn and create consciously enables us to expand and maximize all our inherent powers. In this sense, learning and creating are our primary powers.

These basic powers, granted a minimally sound mind and body, are bestowed upon every human being as a birthright. That said, it is not necessarily the case that every individual will fully exercise his or her birthright of power. This is the unfortunate situation of the grownup throughout every stratum of society. For some, these limits are set by family; for others, they are set by society itself. There are many people in our communities who receive continual messages that they are inadequate, unworthy, and unequal. The messages of prejudice, poverty, and violence, when delivered continuously, create an almost insurmountable barrier to the experience of personal power.

Adults whose powers have not been interfered with like to learn. They have been able to preserve a child's natural curiosity, as well as a child's capacity for pleasurable absorption in a task. Adults like the sensation of their mind working, their hands working, their body working—the fluent expression of their creativity, intelligence, and ability to communicate. Adults enjoy challenges and the efforts they inspire. They enjoy the feeling of accomplishment and their own success. They deal with failure comfortably: Failure is simply information in the process of mastery and learning.

Mistakes don't define the adult. This doesn't mean that adults aren't disappointed or discouraged by their mistakes. Rather, they expect these feelings as part of the process, especially when the task being attempted has meaning and passion associated with it. Adults know when rest is needed, and when it's time to take a break. They also know the importance of play and spontaneity—in terms of bringing fresh, new energy and ideas to their work, as well as resting from it.

Adults have preserved or recaptured the playful, inventive, spontaneous quality of well-loved children. Most of us have these adult powers, albeit muted and stultified to some degree by the grownup's forced exile from spontaneity and joy.

Power and Validation

For the adult, the exercise of personal power is self-validating. In other words, the experience of exercising one's power or ability is in itself sufficient to confer validation and meaning, regardless of whether a specific result is produced. Grownups, on the other hand, must have their power constantly validated by others and must be able to measure it in terms of results. The power is experienced not in the conscious capacity to flex the muscle but in being able to lift a certain amount of weight. Grownups, because of their disconnection both from their internal world and an internal, self-validating "I," are forced to look outside themselves for validation of their power. Their operating principle is *I have power only when I control, dominate, or win.* They are unable to experience their power from the inside.

The adult's use of power as directed by an internal "I" is well illustrated by what happened to a friend of ours. Alice is a political strategist. She has developed the successful campaign strategies by which many candidates have won office. Driving to work one day with her husband, Alice was struck by how depressed she felt. Her low energy worried her, because she was presenting a campaign strategy to a new client that morning and had depended on feeling as excited and powerful as she had all week while preparing it. "In the past," she told us, "I would have had more coffee, ignored the down feelings, and told myself 'Grow up! You've just got the jitters.' Instead, since I know better by now, I looked back on the morning and the previous evening to see if there was anything there I should be paying attention to. *Why bother?* was a phrase that kept rolling around in my head. That I was hearing it was a clue, even though I couldn't understand why I was hearing it this time. Then I remembered the call I had gotten the previous evening from a friend. He told me that a former client, a candidate from whose campaign I had resigned, was going to get off in an investigation I had hoped would bring his illegal use of finances to light. When I worked for this man, he was not only dishonest, but abused his power in other ways as well. When I left, I'd warned some friends of mine in the office about what was going on; but to my surprise, they were angry at me for rocking the boat, and remain cool and dismissive of me to this day. My leftover anger about that really unpleasant experience left me wanting to see him get caught and have to pay. I guess there were a few people I wanted to say 'I told you so' to.

"The feeling of being closed out and seen as the troublemaker was unpleasantly familiar from my childhood. I had never been vindicated in my family for the power of my role as truthteller, and there was still a raw wound there which erupted into my morning when I realized I was still going to be seen as the bad guy, and this real-life bad guy was going to get away with his crimes. The weight of my history fell on me then, and I felt victimized all over again.

"As we drove along, I told my husband what was going on for me. When I finished, he reminded me that I had not been powerless in that political situation with my former boss. I had taken care of myself and prevented myself from being associated with an unscrupulous politician, even though it meant the loss of some people's esteem. My husband also reminded me that even though I was shaky in the power of my self-validation at the moment, I still clearly believed in myself, my values, and my abilities. Hearing that turned the experience of the morning around. I was able to reconnect with the reality of my power instead of to the feeling of powerlessness. I knew that my worried feelings and memories could do nothing to diminish my real power. That comes from inside me, and no one can touch that."

It is worth noticing the whole sequence of adult powers that Alice was able to call upon. First, she knows that her inner life influences her. This knowledge is powerful, allowing her to pause and notice how she was being influenced by her feelings and vague worries. She did not have to deny, ignore, or manipulate the information they gave her. In fact, she used that information to look further into her experience. She was able to share what was going on with a trusted friend. Her ability to trust not only herself but her husband put her in a powerful position to get and use feedback. She had the power of an inner consciousness of her value, and the ability to act on it without regard to what others might think of her actions. She was able to experience how the past was different from the present, and from that knowledge to guide her reactions and behavior. She saw how she stood alone in the present and yet felt validated in contrast to how standing alone in the past had made her feel canceled.

Alice exercised all these powers in the space of an hour's commute to her job. As an adult, she knows that the greatest power she has is her ability to stay with the process of looking inside in order to fully understand how outside events are affecting her. Her commitment and persistence are powerful, too. They are in fact amalgams of all the powers she has found in herself and claimed over the years. They are born from the power to choose. Her adult ability to validate her own learning process and choices, despite other people who might see her as flawed, allows her to use her powers to the fullest.

Learning and Power

Adult lives are about learning and dealing creatively with growth and change. Our two greatest powers are the ability to learn and the ability to create. These powers are interior processes that determine the quality and effectiveness of our lives. Because they are part of the inner life, the grownup's access to them is limited. Each of the powers available to us is further powered by our ability to learn. Human powers and abilities evolve over time in every individual, becoming more refined. They are uniquely defined and expressed by the person using them. This evolution could not take place in the absence of our power to learn. Without this power, all our potential remains just that—potential. It cannot be said strongly enough that a conscious, intentional use of our ability to learn is the critical factor in the realization of our powers.

It may seem a strange thing to say, but many people simply cannot learn. Grownups have been raised to believe that their limits are flaws. They fear not knowing, and they're terrified of making mistakes. Underneath the superficial acknowledgment that they are "only human," they believe that being a real adult means always being an expert. Not knowing is emotionally equated with inadequacy and immaturity.

But human beings are learning machines. This has always seemed intuitively true and is now being borne out by the latest findings in neurophysiology. We master our powers by trial and error. A child learns to walk by falling a lot until she's moved by the impulse to put out a foot and stop the fall forward, and when this works, she puts out the other foot, and so staggers on until she's walking.

Powers are dormant within all mammals, developing over time with the maturation of the body, the growth of experience and skills, and the training and modeling of caregivers. Much of this development can take place without the presence of a conscious, self-reflecting "I" in either the teacher or the student. This is how it works in all animals except human beings, so far as we know. Animal spheres of activity and influence are narrowly circumscribed, whereas for human beings the possibilities are vast.

Because of our inherent freedom to move our awareness around at will, both inside and outside ourselves, we can enter more and broader spheres of influence and activity than other mammals. The flexibility of that reflective, aware, internal "I," combined with the power of our intellect, lets us not only think thoughts but also "watch" our own thought processes, allowing us to learn from our own thinking as we think. That aware "I," combined with the power of our creativity, can deliberately project a vexing question onto our internal screen and watch as our imagination produces a fresh, new solution. Combined with the information from an emotion, that "I" can intentionally feel its way into the meaning a given event or person has for us and then produce a meaningful response. That "I" can interact with the body in increasingly refined and powerful ways to produce startling athletic or artistic results. In her book *Real Power*, Janet Hagbert writes: "Personal power at the highest stage includes the power derived from external sources . . . but combines that with the power that can be derived only from within." We agree.

There is very little acceptance in our culture that young people are capable of discovering and maintaining that kind of learning relationship with themselves or the world around them. There is much more emphasis on training young people to avoid making mistakes—perhaps because the grownups teaching them experience such anguish over their own mistakes, past, present, and future.

A lot of grownups learn on the run or accidentally, if they learn at all. When we are in our grownup state, we don't notice that we are learning—we are just doing. Learning is not a deliberate, conscious choice or experience. This shortsightedness preserves the grownup's fantasy that he or she "knew it already," and keeps in place the belief that not knowing is bad and shameful.

We have all had the experience of agonizing over a choice, looking for the right answer, the one that will not be a mistake. Caught in these miserable binds—Should I? Shouldn't I?—the grownup has no sense that a mistake and its accompanying lesson could be interesting or expanding, and might even result in a better outcome. A grownup's identity rests on making the right choice in the first place. Mistakes are seen as irremediable wrong turns. Because we're so focused on results rather than process, it's difficult to see the possible usefulness of the path a mistake might take us on, even if we wind up at the same place we would have gone directly if we'd made another choice. For example, an unwise early marriage may be seen as a mistake. But the path of those years—even if it contains suffering—may confer the experience and wisdom needed to create a second marriage founded on good sense and self-respect.

All our educational training is focused on "getting it right." But making mistakes is an essential part of learning. To create an ideal atmosphere for learning, we need to be trained in kindness toward ourselves as we live by trial and error, and in the valuing of our false moves and wrong choices. Being angry at ourselves or hating ourselves for our failings is as wrong-headed as getting mad at the baby who is trying so hard, through stumbling and falling, to learn to walk. Trying to be our best selves is a lifelong process that mirrors the baby's step-by-step progress. Like the baby, we need encouragement for our efforts, congratulations for our successes, and admiration for getting up and starting again when we fall.

The experience of learning for the grownup is one of having to get it right the first time. It is a matter of emergency prevention, in which bad consequences surround all choices. Even though grownups readily admit that mistakes happen, their behavior belies a powerful need to hide them. Grownup behavior around mistakes is full of excuses, defenses, rationalization, indecision, fabrications, exaggerations, minimizations, cover-up, damage control, attack, sulking, silences, and clichés. All of this is the grownup's attempt to protect his or her self-image. So much of the grownup's energy is tied up in these protective strategies that there is little energy left over for learning or creativity.

Learning Versus Training

In business as well as personal situations, experimentation is seen as a frightening alternative. The way it's been done before becomes the only safe way. This condition is under intense scrutiny now in American organizations and businesses, since the marketplace is demanding that they learn more quickly, and be more consistently creative, or be blown off the playing field. James F. Moore, a management consultant writing in the *Harvard Business Review*, May/June 1993, notes, "For most companies today the only sustainable competitive advantage comes from out-innovating the competition." In "The Tom Peters Seminar" book, Tom Peters, a widely respected leader in organizational development, quotes a leading business executive as saying, "Strategies are okayed in boardrooms that even a child would say are bound to fail. The problem is, there's never a child in the boardroom."

There is a difference between learning and training. The grownup is more the result of training, and the adult is more the result of learning. Training has mostly to do with obeying, memorizing, and behaving in a prescribed way. In training, we are given content and expected to absorb, imitate, memorize, and then regurgitate the material. All the answers are known. Training does not require self-awareness or any input from the trainee. It requires only the desire to avoid pain and seek pleasure (in other words, the desire to avoid making mistakes and to win approval for getting it right). Training alters a person's behavior whereas learning alters the person. Unlike learning, training can be accomplished with the lights on but nobody at home.

Learning requires a person's conscious presence. The

grownup, exclusively focused on external reality, is exiled from this experience—and *exile* is the operative word, because the realm of learning is one in which we all were once at home as children. If I am here, as fully present as I can be from moment to moment, in the very process of mastering something my self-awareness is changing, expanding, becoming more refined, strengthened, known, and valued.

Most grownups have trouble registering changes in themselves, and some grownups simply cannot do it, because they are incapable of experiencing the process of mastery from the inside. Another accomplishment may be notched onto the grownup's belt, but it has not been consciously recorded in his or her inner bank account. This is why so many accomplished grownups feel empty and unfulfilled at the end of a project—or at the end of their life.

In the conscious process of learning, we search out, explore, distinguish, analyze, and choose where and how to place information inside ourselves, whether or not to act on it, and how it relates to the world around us. Such learning requires self-awareness. It is essential in the adult learning process to attend to our internal responses to the material coming in and to be able to learn from them. For example, we can register fear if we are afraid about the ways in which new information may challenge deeply held pet theories or our accustomed self-image. This enables us to consider the part of us that is afraid, to do whatever is necessary to dispel that fear, and, as a result, to open ourselves to new possibilities. Learning includes our inner reactions and may involve understanding new things about ourselves. There is a sort of dialogue between the student and the material to be learned, which includes constant reflection. When true learning is taking place, these dialogues are a process of discovering answers and insights, rather than one of reading maps to particular and predictable destinations.

It is an adult power to be able to entertain this type of learning dialogue, putting up with the temporary murkiness, uncertainty, chaos, and flux of the unresolved state of not knowing yet. This process of learning can accommodate both mistakes and successes and is open to all sorts of innovative knowledge and behavior.

Yet there is a place for training in learning, when it is consciously chosen to produce a certain benefit. For the most part, though, training is hierarchical and goal-oriented and is mostly about behavior and outer appearances. Because when learning is forced, it can remove the sense of value we get from the process. In this kind of training, we obey the same clichés that spring from our grownup education: Don't rock the boat!, Let sleeping dogs lie!, Grow up!, and Toe the line!

In his book *The Fifth Discipline*, Peter Senge describes the adult's approach to learning when he talks about "personal mastery." He writes: "People with a high level of personal mastery . . . have learned how to perceive and work with forces of change rather than resist those forces. They are deeply inquisitive . . . They feel connected to others and to life itself. They feel as if they are part of a larger creative process, which they can influence but cannot unilaterally control.

"People with a high level of personal mastery live in a continual learning mode. They never 'arrive' . . . It is a lifelong discipline . . . [they] are acutely aware of their ignorance, their incompetence, their growth areas. And they are deeply self-confident. Paradoxical? Only for those who do not see the 'The journey is the reward.'"

The Power of Creativity

Our other primary power is the power to create. Like the power to learn, it becomes manifest through our other powers (thinking, expressing, moving, intuiting, and so on). Everybody is creative, although not everyone is necessarily artistic. (See Cameron, 1992; Fritz, 1984; and Ray and Myers, 1989, in the bibliography for some wonderful methods for reconnecting with and releasing your creativity.)

Creativity has too long been identified with being artistic—in other words, with using your creativity to make art. This is a wonderful and powerful way to use creativity, but far from the only way.

You are creating all the time. You just take it for granted. Think about it. Who creates (brings into being) the thoughts in your mind, the movement in your body, the sounds from your vocal chords, the ways in which you arrange your living space or your desk, the choice of clothes you buy and wear, the food you put on the table, the look of your signature, the recipes you make up, the letters you write, the way you plant and care for your garden, your solutions for getting the kids from here to there, the expressions of love you show your mate, the jokes you tell, the unique spin you put on a story? Whether or not you can take credit for the creativity involved, nobody else is inside you creating but yourself.

Creative energy is a mystery in that it cannot be directly observed. It can be witnessed only in its effects. It's sort of like the wind—you can't see it, but you can see everything it moves. By effects, we don't mean only outside products, such as pieces of art or new inventions, but inside products as well: ideas, solutions to problems, ways of moving, making sounds, visualizing, or imagining particular things.

Tapping into your creative power is a bit like standing beside a well and sending the bucket (question, curiosity, problem, desire) down into the unknown darkness of possibility. You may haul up a terrific answer to your question, a reward for your curiosity, a solution to your problem, the fulfillment of your desire, or a bucketful of new questions. Sometimes the exercise of creativity is more like sitting next to a geyser like Old Faithful, waiting for the next eruption of ideas, solutions, insights, and so on. The spouting of the geyser is not something you can force, but your internal "I"—your intimate witness—can be in a state of readiness to see it, to watch it carefully each time, and grow to be on such intimate terms with it that you are always able to ride the crest of its energy when it surges. Some additional resources on creative energy and using it include *The Creative Spirit* (Goleman, Kaufman, and Ray, 1992) and an audiotape by Clarissa Pinkola Estes called *The Creative Fire*. (These resources are included in the bibliography at the end of the book.)

Creativity is ordinarily associated only with bringing something new and original into being—an idea, solution, product, design, theory, and so on. Creativity's capacity to do this is its major contribution to humankind. The experience of creative energy moving through you and producing something new that is beautiful or useful or both is deeply thrilling. The process of preparation, incubation, reflection/dreaming, and illumination involved in the creative cycle is described well in *The Creative Spirit*.

But this book and many others limit the definition of creativity to the production of something original. We don't think that any standard should ever be imposed that would mask or invalidate an individual's creative output, whatever its form.

Such standards only disempower people, in the same way that becoming famous has grown to be the standard of success for all "serious" creative endeavor. Writing a poem is a successful act of creation. Getting it published is something else altogether and has as much to do with luck, status, and marketing skills as it does with creativity. Your choice of curtains for the living room may not affect as many people as Henri Matisse's choice of color in one of his paintings, but the act of choosing for both you and Matisse involved the exact same type of spiritual and esthetic resources.

Creativity is an amalgam of skills and longings that are sometimes galvanized in response to dissatisfaction with things as they are, and sometimes out of a desire to celebrate things as they are. It is often a spontaneous, unconscious response—an outgrowth of play or fun, for example—which you recognize as new, and value as such, only later, after reflection.

Creativity operates in the dialogue established between a desire and its fulfillment. Before fulfillment comes, the creative process is characterized by trial and error, periods of confusion and discouragement, surprise, blankness, activity, revision, critical contemplation, despair, and finally trust that the original idea is working its way through the layers of the process to emerge as your best effort to express something authentically and truthfully. Trust is a crucial element. It requires acknowledgment of your partnership with the unknown within you, over which you have no control.

Like learning, creativity requires the presence of an internal intimate witness—the adult "I"—to fully tap into its power. If I cannot turn my awareness inward, where creativity lives (as so many grownups cannot), then I'm not in a position to receive its gifts. If I've learned to be frightened and condemning of major aspects of myself, my access to my creativity will be severely limited at best, if not entirely blocked. For creativity to thrive, we must be in contact with the adult "I" and be willing to experience whatever comes up.

Creative energy seems to do its best work at the cutting edge, where things are unknown, fresh, new, different, and often risky. The adult self knows that this is okay and enriching. Adults understand that nothing inside them is really dangerous, even though some things may feel absolutely terrifying and may need to be approached slowly and with respect.

Creativity is a neutral power in that it can be applied in destructive as well as constructive ways—for example, in figuring out how to infiltrate a computer system, or ways to commit genocide efficiently or build houses over a toxic-waste dump. It's not good or bad in itself; it simply is. In fact, creativity can be used to stifle creativity—used against itself. Grownups have been taught to fear their creative energy, except when it is applied to maintaining the status quo. It is paradoxical to think of creativity used for *preventing* change, but consider the creativity of grownups in coming up with rationalizations that allow them to maintain their unconsciousness about themselves and their harmful behaviors.

The defense mechanism called denial provides a good illustration. As in any defense, the need is to avoid consciousness of a certain feared reality—perhaps some accurate but critical bit of feedback or an embarrassing mistake. To accomplish the escape into oblivion, you have to shift the focus of your awareness away from the feared reality and create an alternative reality—a fantasy, a story, an excuse, or a novel interpretation.

One of Lou's clients remembers as a ten-year-old kid being caught by his mother with the smell of cigarette smoke on his breath. She went into a terrifying rage and threatened him with dire consequences. In his panic, he told her, "My breath always smells that way—really! You can ask the dentist's assistant. She said it to me the last time I was there." Although unconvincing as an explanation, it was an outrageous bit of creativity, and startled his mother so much that she forgot about punishing him.

The point is, creative power can be put to any use, including bringing about its own demise. Many people do this by making up the story that they are not creative, not playful, not spontaneous, and telling it to themselves over and over again until they make it real—until they're completely convinced by their own fabrication. Kids are forced to do this by parents and teachers who have been taught to fear their own uniqueness, spontaneity, dreams, and playfulness. Creativity comes from your innermost self. If the inner sanctum has had to be shut down for reasons of safety and self-protection, much of your creative power in the present will be tied up in keeping the doors securely locked. Nothing will be left over for generative creativity.

Like consciousness, creativity is highly adaptable. It can be called upon to assist with anything: robbing a bank, painting a picture, telling yourself phony stories (rationalizations), self-criticism, designing buildings, inventing gadgets or tools, fighting a war, shrinking or expanding your contact with your senses, running an organization, baking bread, writing a book. Creativity is like fire in that it transforms whatever it touches. It is like electricity in that it generates connections, shedding light where there was only darkness before, and making things move.

Reclaiming Your Power

If there were no such thing as change, we would never need to develop our latent powers. But change is inevitable in every aspect of our lives. It is empowering to be able to accept that fact and deploy your creativity in an adult relationship to change. Jung says it well in his *Collected Works:* "All true things must change, and only that which changes remains true."

The grownup is programmed to try to prevent change, or at least to keep it under control. This need triggers a powerful process of denial. Adults are in touch with their power to grow and change in harmony with the events and opportunities around them, living in the moment as it is, rather than getting stuck living in the moment as they wish it was.

There are many places along the way at which your power to change can be derailed. For example, you may become aware at some point of reliving a traumatic event or situation from the past. Take, for example, the woman who has decided to deal with her eating problems. She suddenly sees the same phenomenon in her daughter or her best friend, panics, and thinks: There's no hope—I'm surrounded! Or the man who wants to deal with his memories of an abusive father, who recognizes with horror the ways in which he abuses his own children.

When you decide to confront and change an unnatural limit in your life, it's important to realize that the limit may assert itself in many different ways, including all the old buried forms in which it manifested itself in the past. Deciding to change something can intensify its grip for a while, or so it feels. At the very least, the limit you are working on seems to appear everywhere. You shouldn't be discouraged if your powers and resolve aren't strong enough to accomplish the change in a given moment. This is a limit in the process of change that needs to be recognized and integrated into the overall process, rather than perceived as a cause for panic and giving up. At this stage, your power lies in recognition, integration, and persistence. At each stage in the changes you want to make, you can firmly plant your feet in the present moment. This is the only place from which you can progress to the next stage.

When you measure your power only by outcomes and results, you lose contact with the range of powers at your disposal, and your self-image and sense of value become dependent on outside events. Even more important, you lose the direct experience of exercising those powers: You feel successful only at the end of a project that turns out the way it was supposed to. When life delivers a blow you're helpless to prevent, you may lose touch with the powers that are available to you by concentrating on your helplessness and sense of failure. It's far more satisfying, realistic, and empowering to measure your success in terms of your ability to move fluidly from moment to moment, adjusting to and re-evaluating your responses to projects or life events as they unfold. The grownup alternative consigns you to suppressing your reactions, limiting yourself to "safe" ways of thinking, and collecting trophies and awards you may have no direct internal experience of deserving and which you constantly fear losing.

There are stages to changing an unnatural and unnecessary internal limit. These stages go something like this:

1. The inner "I" notices a desire for some new, better, or more fulfilling way of being in the world. Most often this desire is highlighted by the experience of some kind of pain or dissatisfaction.

2. From my innermost perspective, I notice and describe as clearly as possible what prevents me from affecting this change, considering both external and internal conditions (for example, attitudes, beliefs, emotions, and so on). This often takes time and a great deal of reflection.

3. I begin the process of eliminating the external obstacles and separating from the internal conditions that unnaturally limit me.

4. When the change starts to show up, I'm ready to deal with its consequences for myself and others—guilt, discomfort, envy, loss, triumph, fear, joy, and so on.

This process was exemplified by a client of Lou's who showed up at his office completely distraught. The man and his girlfriend had been mugged at knifepoint in the subway in New York City. In his therapy session, the man, who we'll call Joe, asked the questions that were tormenting him. "Why does God allow this?" he wanted to know. "What is the lesson to be learned here? Is God sadistic, and if He isn't, why would something like this take place? I feel like I am supposed to figure this out, and God isn't giving me any clues. If He would just let me know the program, maybe I could act accordingly." This was Joe's initial response to being dominated and violated by an outside force which he had no power to counteract. Joe was in the first stage of changing an internal limit: recognizing his pain. Stage two—noticing and describing what prevents change—was soon to follow.

The confrontation with limits can be a means for discovering our true power. What emerged from therapy was how Joe had given up his own power to think the experience through for himself and to feel his feelings about it. He was so preoccupied with trying to figure out what God "meant" by the mugging that he was ignoring his own internal experience of its impact—his feelings of helplessness, fear, vulnerability, shame, rage, and pain. He was behaving in classic grownup style in reaction to an experience that shook his image of himself as being in control. He was subtly blaming God for the event, because somewhere below the surface of his awareness he feared that he himself was to blame—and, for a grownup, such feelings are intolerable. A scapegoat must be found.

When grownups experience a real emergency, their thoughts are captured in the present by the unconscious need to deny their internal responses. Thinking in this context serves to keep feeling at bay. This type of thinking is not about learning or understanding. It is about manipulating the facts of the event to make you look like you're in charge, or at least not to blame. When life has dealt us a blow and demonstrated that we are not in control, it is natural to react with fear. Our grownup need to avoid feeling afraid can cause us to deny or minimize real and present danger.

And yet the reality is that when we are overpowered in a situation, our power lies in knowing that we are out of control, and operating out of that awareness. This might mean protecting ourselves, feeling extremely uncomfortable, feeling afraid, running away, or whatever response is appropriate to our sense of being overpowered. Many a recovering battered woman wishes she had been able, *before* she got hurt, to let in the awareness that her situation was out of her control.

After an experience of having been rendered powerless, our power lies in our ability to process what has happened to us without self-recrimination or blame. Joe was consumed by self-criticism and judgment after the mugging. "I should have seen it coming," he said. "I should have put up a fight." When the grownup is in charge of the events of our lives and responding from the belief that our limits are flaws, we blame ourselves for being out of control. Remember, the grownup operating principle is *I have power only when I control, dominate, or win.* So in a situation in which we are physically or psychically overpowered, we are left with our sense of power fundamentally invalidated.

Joe was confusing power with dominance. Once he became aware of being stuck in grownup thinking, he was able to claim what belonged to him—the ability to learn—to look at the facts of the situation and see that he had no control over preventing the mugging from happening. He was now in stage three of changing an unnatural limit. Shifting back to using his awareness to collect the data of his own internal experience, he reconnected with the fact that he had been violated and felt anger, fear, and humiliation—especially that he hadn't been able to protect his girlfriend. Revisiting stage two, he also saw his own powerlessness in the face of these emotions, and his shame in feeling that way. He wanted to cover up both his responses to the mugging and his responses to his responses. Rather than deal with the experience of feeling powerless, he kept going off into considerations about God. His grownup self found it difficult to let the feelings be, accept all his reactions, and know that he could, if he chose, learn to respond to them differently. He used his powers of understanding to know that it would take time and acceptance to feel both his adult and his grownup responses simultaneously and to eventually shift the balance of power in favor of the adult.

Joe finally understood that he had experienced a real emergency in the mugging and that his grownup self had needed to avoid emotional contact with that reality because of an unhealed wound from the past. He was able to touch that wound with the healing awareness of his adult and move back into a place of contact with his personal power. This was stage two for Joe.

Joe's defensive thoughts did nothing to clue him in to his avoidance of his deeper internal experience. In any other context, his questions about his relationship to God would have been valid ones to ask. Sometimes, though, your thoughts are a poor indicator of the state you're in. In fact, the grownup state often co-opts your thoughts, using them to shout down or otherwise obscure your instincts and feelings. For Joe, the question of responsibility was transformed into a program of managing blame.

At such times, your body is a better indicator than your thoughts about the purpose of your thinking. When you're involved in the effort to deny something you feel—in an emergency prevention response—there is tension in the body: Your muscles are tightly held and your breathing is shallow. Fear and worry are present in that state, and you feel a sense of urgency. Such feelings sound an alarm inside you, indicating the presence of an old wound. Paying attention to the alarm can help you shift the balance of power from your grownup to your adult.

A means of stepping away from the swirl of defensive thinking is to simplify the field of your awareness and concentrate only on your breathing for a short time. This entails pausing and paying careful attention to the breath, watching it go in and out, and gradually letting your breaths become longer and deeper. Your internal "I" is shifting the focus of its attention; thoughts and emotions tend to quiet down. When this happens, you can relax into your body and begin to listen to what's really going on inside. You bring your "I" awareness down into your body and separate from the internal limiting condition of driven, defensive thinking. This internal action opens you to conscious contact with the full range of your powers. Tuning in like this can give you a truer picture of what your options are and how to exercise them.

When Joe's breathing became more relaxed, he was able to analyze his reactions to the mugging. He was more open to Lou's questions and began to formulate questions of his own, which were more geared to his personal experience, and the information embedded in it, than to abstruse philosophical musings.

Surviving Versus Thriving

Adults use creativity, learning, and all their inherent powers to thrive, rather than just survive. In *Webster's* dictionary, *survive* is basically defined as outliving someone else or continuing to exist or live "after or in spite of"; *thrive* is defined as to prosper or flourish, to grow vigorously or luxuriantly. These are very different states—in fact, they're diametrically opposed. If your basic internal state is one of survival, your experience will be one of "continuing to exist in spite of." If your internal state is one of thriving, your internal experience will be one of "flourishing, growing vigorously and luxuriantly." When you are powerless and your survival is threatened by someone, your creativity and learning are applied to surviving.

When a parent threatens a child's sense of self by refusing to accept her feelings or way of thinking or being, her creativity will be directed toward removing the threat. Since the child is powerless to change the parent's attitude and behavior, creativity and learning must be applied to destroying or hiding herself. She will disengage from the offending muscles, she will think the thoughts the parent wants her to, she will smile—or cry—if that is what's required, she will act as if she doesn't care or didn't do it, she will pretend she doesn't know what she passionately *does* know. The child will become an expert in her own particular war zone and in surviving her own situation. The more extensively the child's creative energy must be focused on surviving, the less creative energy there will be to help that child grow and thrive. These defenses are carried into adulthood and lived until consciously changed.

Being motivated to thrive instead of survive is a completely different mind-set reflecting a completely different internal state. Surviving means getting away with your life: You are on the edge of extinction or some other cataclysmic disaster. Surviving is getting out alive. It assumes a threat, an enemy—something you have to fight and eliminate in order to get what you need to survive. This may be something somebody else has, such as food or air or water. Or it may be the need to disarm an enemy, to take away their gun, or their knife, or the open hand they slap you with, or the words with which they abuse you. Winning in a survival situation means taking something away from someone else. It's an adversarial lifestyle built on threat and shortage.

Grownups believe in the power of survival of the fittest to winnow out the weak and defective and produce greatness—to keep them on their toes, to keep them motivated, to keep them moving. They avoid letting down their guard for fear of growing slack, of losing their edge. They don't know how to become motivated in the absence of some sort of threat, real or imagined, internal or external. We are deeply programmed to operate in the domain of survival—genetically, physically, familially, socially, and economically.

If the reasons necessitating a survival stance disappear, does the motivation for thriving automatically take their place? What is the motivation behind the urge to thrive? Beyond being pleasure-driven, the urge to thrive also has an intense spiritual component. It's about discovering your wholeness. It's about increasing your vibrancy and the richness of your experience. It's about strengthening your connection with yourself and others. It's expansive and open. The goals of survival, on the other hand, are about gaining dominance, making sure you have enough, eliminating threat, expanding your control, weakening the power of others, decreasing their share, and hoarding.

If you knew absolutely and without doubt that your survival, internal and external, was not threatened, what would that feel like? What would move you? What would interest you? What might you do that you don't do now? What might you stop doing that you do now? What might you add to or subtract from the ways in which you move through your life? What would you stop worrying about? In what new ways would you be free to enjoy yourself?

Power and Identity

So many of us either take our powers for granted or don't have a sense of ownership of them, or, at worst, are hostile to them. Being conscious of your personal power does not mean simply using it. It means being aware in the moment that it is *your* power and that *you* are using it. It means feeling the power in your own hands, so to speak, and then choosing how you exercise it.

This is the source of the responsibility associated with enlightened power. When you are deeply aware of your inner self, it's unnatural to blank out and commit outrages against others.

Evil is something that can be generated only out of a blocked or killed self-awareness. You are not drawn to destroy or mutilate when you have the connections to life generated by an intimate self-awareness and knowledge of your own power.

This reaffirms the fundamental importance of being in contact with that internal sense of "I." How can you have an experience of your powers if you don't have an internal awareness that you are exercising them? If you can't feel your muscles or your emotions, sense your intuition, witness and direct your thoughts and creativity, find and hear your voice, how can you know your innermost realities? How can you learn?

The powers you are allowed to exercise and own were allotted to you by your family of origin. Reclaiming the powers you had to give up involves becoming aware of your grownup training and the defenses you put in place to protect yourself and then carefully dismantling them. This reclamation process depends on your internal sense of safety and separateness as codified in the first two operating principles of adulthood. It is about having the inner authority to do this, as well as the inner power.

Many if not most people have lost a lot of their powers and abilities by the end of their adolescence. It can be a revelation to realize that there is more to you than the self-definition you carried into adulthood, that there are parts of you that you buried young and parts of you that never saw the light of day. But even following this type of revelation, an inner alienation and sense of constriction can persist. So many people have said to us something like, "I can see the rest of me, but I just can't touch it, can't take it in my 'inside' hands and feel it and hold it and say, 'This is mine.'"

As noted in chapter 2, children are not born with a fully developed inner capacity or authority to self-define. Like the motor skill of walking, self-definition must evolve and reveal itself. For most of us, this power is never allowed to develop unimpeded; we are not given the acceptance or level of safety required. Most of us are more or less *told* who we are by our parents and educators and are left to work out our lives and identities around that definition. We are given a picture of ourselves that is inaccurate in its limited potential and level of negative labeling, whether we submit to or rebel against it. Since this "me" is the only one we ever get to know and experience, we become very attached to it, very identified with it. Even if it frustrates us or causes us pain, the notion of losing it or giving it up is terrifying. It is the equivalent on the physical level of telling someone, "Your body is an illusion—just let it go."

The Choice to Be Powerful

When asked "Who are you?" people usually answer with a description of what they do. The essential "I-ness" of each individual cannot be boiled down to a word or two, because we are each so complex. You can sometimes get an immediate take on someone, especially if you are in a particularly receptive state—for example, in loving intimacy. But it usually takes an enormous effort of expression, observation, and shared experience before one person can truly know another, or even for one person to gain a deep level of self-knowledge. As we described it in chapter 3, an enlightened sense of "I" would reflect an inner experience of self that has to do with simply being, not doing or having. It would answer the question, "Who are you?" with the words, "I am" or, possibly, "I am I."

To redefine who you are, you have to bypass the partial, limited sense of self that has accompanied you from childhood, especially if that self has been defined as powerless or uncreative. The best that grownups can do is work on their outer appearance, making themselves over in the outer realms: They get better at who they already are, what they already know, or how they already appear. But they're unable to touch the exiled parts of themselves. This is precisely the grownup paradigm and the inherent limit that paradigm presents in any grownup program of self-improvement.

One of the major pitfalls for grownups is that new information, which could help them recover their powers and redefine their sense of self, goes into the emergency prevention response system that is already in place. As such, it must be acted on immediately, possessed, and controlled—or else it risks becoming further evidence of inadequacy. This complicates the process of claiming your powers, because every piece of knowledge that might reconnect you is a potential accusation demanding even more damage control. Information itself becomes a threat in this system.

Through a combination of creativity and learning, you can expand your internal contact with skills you would like to develop. For example, pick some interpersonal skill or behavior you would like to master. Pick something that fits with your values. Now imagine a character who is really good at this skill, who practices it easily and with confidence. He or she can be real or fictional, or a new you. Picture this person being the way you want to be, acting how you would like to act, with ease. Notice where inside yourself you are doing this imagining. Notice that it is you who is doing it. Feel as much as possible what it would feel like to be this person with this skill. Feel your way into this person's skin and thought processes. You can also notice how this seems different from or similar to how you think and feel now. The next time you are in a situation in which this skill would be useful, imagine your character and feel what it is like to be him or her in the situation. What would the character do that might not be possible for you? How would it feel to be able to do that? Try one small gesture or behavior your character would naturally do, and watch how it affects the rest of your behavior and the feeling of being yourself inside your skin.

We all possess tremendous powers, whether we choose to claim them or not. Each one of us is like the citizen who has the right to vote but doesn't exercise that right. Even if you are unconscious of your power, or indifferent to it, or ignore or refuse to exercise it, you are still choosing. Not acting, not thinking, not taking responsibility—all are choices that allow the status quo to remain unchanged. We are not talking about the value of the status quo, but about the fact that our power is a fluid energy in us, which will exist whether we choose to channel it or not. Adults make a choice to move into conscious contact with the energy of power flowing through them.

Contacting the Internal Power Source

Here is an exercise you can use to expand your contact with your internal powers.

Find a quiet place and sit comfortably. Take a series of deep breaths, letting your awareness drop inside your chest and belly along with your breath. Now, bring to mind a problem that has been bothering you. Hold this problem in your awareness without "trying" to fix it.

What is one emotion you connect with this problem? Bring your awareness to the feel of this emotion and see what information it gives you about the problem.

Now, with your awareness still focused within, ask your intuition for an insight about this problem. Take whatever comes.

Then, still using your breath as an internal focus, ask your imagination for an image or idea about this problem.

Finally, still keeping the focus of your attention within, ask your body how it would like to move in response to this problem. Now just be with whatever information or experiences you have had for a few moments. Don't strain to make sense of it. Just be aware of it all.

As a way of furthering your contact with what you have discovered, write down everything so that you can return to contemplate it later.

Keep bringing your awareness to the problem periodically in this fashion until it resolves or dissolves. Each time, make sure to consciously note the internal powers you use to explore and resolve this problem.

CHAPTER NINE

I Always Have Limits

"I . . . find it fascinating that baseball, alone in sport, considers errors to be part of the game, part of its rigorous truth."
—Francis T. Vincent, Commissioner of Baseball

If we are capable of so much as conscious human beings, what are the limits to our personal power? Obviously, we face limits set by the physical world. A paraplegic, no matter how conscious, cannot hope to be a dancer. A man—at least at this point in time—cannot realistically aspire to give birth to a child. Past a certain age, no one has a snowball's chance in hell of being an Olympic athlete. But physical or environmental limits have little to do with how seriously limited most people feel. What are those other limits that keep us from feeling fulfilled in our lives?

Limits to an individual's personal power can be broken down into three basic categories:

- physical or absolute limits
- limits pertaining to skills or aptitude
- limits that are psychologically induced

Physical or absolute limits are the easiest to explain: Your body will not go through a wall, your eyes cannot see around corners, your ears are unable to hear certain sounds. A friend, knowing the limits of her time and lifetime, and all the things she would like to accomplish and experience, expressed her wish to evade these limits: "I know it's impossible, but I could use three concurrently running lives."

Any limits you experience in relationship to a particular skill or aptitude are actually momentary limits. Every such limit is subject to change. The Olympic athlete was once performing at a lower level. Everyone has to start somewhere. You might not ever achieve the highest level of skill in any endeavor—all you can hope to achieve is the highest level of skill you can manage, given your physical and absolute limits in the situation. If you begin ballet classes as an adult, you probably should not expect to become the prima ballerina in a major dance company—although this *could* happen in the absence of physical limits. If you set out to learn eleven foreign languages, you are limited only by your time and level of persistence, barring any organic limits to your ability. If you are in your adult mode and constantly learning, skill limits are in constant flux. There is no absolute here: You are capable of achieving wonders. The key is in knowing that in any given moment *there always will be limits to what you can do and achieve:* this is a condition of being human, not a problem subject to resolution.

Unlike physical limits or time-based limits in skill, psychological limits immobilize potentially vital aspects of your personal power, making those aspects unavailable to you. For example, a person with a phobia of the water has within her the power or ability to learn to swim, but that power is effectively nullified by the phobia. Another example is the internal relationship to yourself that is characterized by the label *low self-esteem.* This means that your perception of yourself is rife with negative, self-hateful, self-deprecating content, which can effectively block your awareness of, and ability to use, your powers. An artist friend of ours was in her sixties before she truly believed that her talent was real. It took numerous shows and plenty of feedback before she could trust her own eyes to perceive the beauty and complexity in her work. "I looked back over work I had done years ago and put away in frustration, thinking it was no good; and it's so good, I am amazed at my own blindness then."

Neurotic fear and depression are also examples of states that limit personal power. From the perspective of someone who is depressed, a whole life can be devalued and dismissed. The feeling of powerlessness in itself can also impose an enormous barrier to the experience and exercise of your personal power. If you are preoccupied with a feeling of powerlessness, you won't be aware of the powers or abilities available to you at any given moment.

You first must be able to conceive of your powers before you can embody them, or to notice them when they are already embodied. Psychologically induced limits to personal power are the bailiwick of the grownup, who chooses to deal with them by denying them, rationalizing them, hiding them, or pretending there's no such thing. Whatever psychologically induced limits we have are the result of early childhood wounds. The beginnings of adult power are in knowing this and allowing the wounds—and the hidden power locked inside them—to emerge from unconsciousness.

We want to distinguish here between *feeling* powerless and *being* powerless. The feeling of powerlessness can rob you of your powers just as effectively as a physical or absolute limit can. Such feelings may or may not correspond to the actual powers available to you at a given point in time. The feeling of powerlessness can coexist with actual power. In all walks of life, there are people who have tremendous power but feel powerless inside.

The grownup rule is basically one of avoiding at all costs the experience of feeling powerless. Grownups are engaged in a constant search for power and, failing that, the illusion of power. To this end, they use whatever evidence they can find and display: social or professional status; conspicuous wealth; one-upmanship; a faultless personal facade (always looking fabulous); a coterie of adoring friends; a "trophy" spouse or lover; a brilliant, beautiful, or immensely talented child; a spotless house; a fancy car; or a prize-winning garden with the biggest tomatoes in town. The point is that grownups will grasp at anything in their effort to build a bulwark against their feelings of powerlessness oozing over the barrier and into the realm of conscious awareness.

There are plenty of business executives who are in fact powerful but feel no claim to that power, with the result that they cannot rest comfortably in their position of authority. They are paranoid about threats to their authority, and are always measuring the power of other people in the organization against their own, always feeling unsafe. Many such people are compelled to demean their subordinates and suck up to their superiors. They're unsure about what it is that confers their own power, so they always have to be on the alert for ways to reinforce it. They don't have the conscious, internal experience of their power, neither in the form of ownership nor exercise. They're missing that "I" that knows their power from the inside. They sense it only when they get good results or in whatever outward status is conferred by their position—how many people work under them, whether their office has a door, or a window, or a view.

The feeling of powerlessness is based on widespread fallacies among individuals about themselves and their capabilities. Robert Fritz, author of *The Path of Least Resistance,* is an expert who has studied creative energy in thousands of people. He says that, with the exception of a handful of people, we are raised to hold one or both of two disempowering, unconscious beliefs. The first is *I am powerless to create what I want;* the second is *I don't deserve to have what I want.* He says—and we agree—that these beliefs act as powerful inhibitors to people's creativity and power, especially because they operate at an unconscious level.

Fritz is describing the grownup. For example, the woman who feels powerless and so stays in an abusive relationship doesn't know, despite a network of supportive family and friends, that she has the power to leave. The man who feels powerless can't leave a job or a career he hates, even though he possesses the power to earn money and find professional fulfillment in countless other ways. The young person who feels powerless can't separate himself from friends who want him to use drugs. These are all examples of people who, for a variety of reasons, have powers they can't use for their own benefit. For all of them, the major impediment is a *feeling* of powerlessness rather than actual powerlessness. When they become aware of their buried powers, they will be amazed at how feasible it would have been all along to leave the abusive relationship, find a new career, or choose to hang out with different friends.

Unconsciousness itself is a major limitation. Grownups are disconnected from their interior reality, which is why they have no contact with the real sources of their power. How can you make a deliberate choice if you're unconscious of the full range of your choices? Dorothy had the ruby slippers all along, but she couldn't access their power until she became aware of it. Until Glinda let her know what was what, they were just a pair of pretty shoes.

A young, very creative woman we know took a job in an ad agency. Her grownup was in charge of her abilities from the first. Karen felt grateful to get the job—as if her abilities had nothing to do with her being hired. The agency was filled with bright people out to prove themselves. Karen had trouble connecting with them, because she didn't see herself as very talented and constantly felt on the defensive. There was a lot of anxiety in the organization, too, which manifested itself as short tempers and screaming deadline meetings and was covered over with bravado and what was called "dedication." The rule in that company was that if you're really dedicated and on the way up, you don't ever say no to extra work, nor do you confront someone who is abusive in their demands for your work.

Karen soon had many people coming to her, saying, "We need your help on this important project." She felt powerless to say no, because she wanted to prove that she was as dedicated as everyone else. Because her professional self-esteem was so low, she also feared being fired (in other words, being rejected). She was easily manipulated into putting in excessively long hours and extra work and was under constant internal pressure to prove her value.

Clearly, Karen was not in contact either with her own powers or the value of her creativity. She was also unable to see how these were both completely separate—and safe—from her work at the ad agency. She measured her value by how many people asked her to work on their projects. Her poor self-image, honed in childhood and adolescence, caused her to need constant reassurance in the present. She didn't know that her power belonged to her rather than to her bosses or colleagues. She did not relate to her power as something she could take with her if she was fired, nor could she imagine taking it someplace where it would be respected.

Karen probably would have stayed on indefinitely at the ad agency if not for the anxiety attacks and asthma that finally forced her, under doctor's orders, to quit. Rather than recognize the enormous power of her creativity, which had put her work so much in demand, she could only see her failure to be tough enough to make it in the dog-eat-dog world of advertising. Karen had never developed an awareness of the first two realities of adulthood: *I am here* and *I am safe.* She was caught in the grownup need to please, a need based in the fear of rejection. Even though the fear was an old one playing itself out in the present, Karen was completely unaware of it or the history that had brought it into being. Because her unconscious grownup persona was in charge of her work life, no amount of praise or admiration from other people could ever convince her that she was "good enough"; and she had too little sense of her own internal "I" to be able to feel with any conviction that she was good enough on her own.

How is it that Karen could have been so unconscious of her considerable powers?

The Sources of Psychologically Induced Limits

Children have a basic need for recognition, validation, and approval. In the areas of power that receive recognition, validation, and approval from parents and caregivers, a particular skill or aptitude is free to develop and thrive. When validation is not given, the development of personal power in general, and specific skills in particular, suffer greatly. When a child's experience or expression of power is threatening to a caregiver, it twists the child's internal connection to that power. At best, this results in an internalized battle to hold on to the power; at worst, it results in the internal suppression of that power. Far from feeling validated, the child feels shamed and abandoned—both intolerable feelings for a youngster. If this happened to you, rather than experience such feelings, you probably became habituated to giving up many areas of power, or things that drew you to them, to the point where you forgot what they were. You certainly would never have had the chance to value these abandoned powers in a way that would allow you to carry them with you into adulthood.

Do any of these statements sound familiar? I can't draw . . . I can't do math . . . I can't sing on key . . . I can't think straight. Many well-meaning parents do horrible damage to their children by hemming them in to limiting and distorted definitions of what and who they are *not*. This can work the other way too. It is just as limiting—and just as damaging—to grow up feeling that you always have to be well-behaved, a good student, gentle, loyal, well organized, or whatever. Both of these narrow ways of defining children create limits that have nothing to do with a child's authentic selfhood, but are rather a product of the parent or caregiver's image of how *they* need the child to be. From a very young age, children are given unspoken rules about which parts of their identity are "okay" and which are not. Certain of the child's powers are eliminated; others may be valued, but only because the parent or caregiver values them.

The grownup's focus in using his or her powers is to please others and avoid abandonment, rather than experience the pleasure and mastery that come with exercising one's power and becoming increasingly skilled at doing so. Our friend Karen, who had to leave the ad agency despite her talent, does not experience the sheer pleasure of mastery. A good first step for her, or for any of us who are not in touch with our power in a given situation, is to ask ourselves the question, *Who* is being creative, reliable, or strong, or exercising this skill? and to answer with facts only. It's also useful to ask: Who or what stops me from using this power? The interior forces (voices, tendencies, aversions, hidden motives, repressed abilities, prohibitions, and so on) that control your ability to exercise power are unnatural limits, created in your past, which nonetheless strongly affect your present reality.

The operating principle of the grownup here is *My limits are either my fault, your fault, or God's fault.* Limits are seen as inherently bad, blameworthy, and shameful: The grownup feels compelled to deny or project them. There is no middle ground of acceptance and awareness. In this context, limits are seen as a function of identity rather than behavior. They aren't recognized as facts reflecting the grownup's present state of knowledge, but as a kind of shameful inheritance and destiny. As such, grownups become disconnected from their own inner adult power to work with their limits by recognizing those that are irrevocable and modifying or overcoming others—to have them, in other words, rather than being had *by* them.

How Limits Affect Our Relationships to Work

The grownup experience of work is very different from the adult experience of work. Even if someone operating more out of the adult side of himself is doing the exact same work as someone operating more out of the grownup side, the experience of working is completely different for them, and there is a good chance that the results of their work will be completely different, too. For a person like Karen, trapped in a largely grownup response, work is rarely about satisfaction or about the exploration of personal power.

Grownups experience work in terms of maintenance or expansion of their sense of control, dominance, and winning. Their hidden agenda is to avoid having their limits exposed. Work for them is rarely about the enjoyment of making a conscious contribution or about the experience of mastery and learning. It is more about the experience of getting through, getting by, continuously proving you're okay and worthwhile, holding on to or expanding your turf (rather than feeling at home there), never being good enough, and therefore having to be perfect. For the grownup, working is about establishing that you exist and controlling the inner experience of emergency, the feeling that you don't count. If a grownup makes a mistake or fails in her work, she experiences this as a sign of danger which must be covered up or fixed in order to prevent another abandonment, another rejection, another experience of shame. If the grownup does well at work—and many do—it's out of a fear-driven motivation that leads to compulsive behaviors, with limited ability to rest, play, or be spontaneous. In terms of working with others, the grownup must either dominate, submit, or isolate. True, comfortable teamwork is not within the realm of possibility for the grownup.

The grownup believes that things should be either/or, not "both/and." This black-and-white outlook is limiting rather than expansive. The adult, on the other hand, can live with paradoxical experiences and conflicting internal states—in fact, the adult knows that mix to be a more accurate model of the way life works. For example, an adult can be comfortable with the knowledge that she is really good at some aspects of her job, and just skilled enough at others. She can see that mixed reality in other people as well, so her expectations are more realistic.

Grownups have been taught to be ashamed of their ignorance or inability. To avoid reexperiencing this shame, they'll go to absurd lengths to avoid having their ignorance revealed. People we've talked to have admitted feeling so much shame at not being omniscient that they'd pretend to know how to give directions to a place they'd never been before. If queried, they'd ad-lib a set of directions that sounded plausible, rather than experience the humiliation of having to say, "Sorry—I don't know."

Adults feel strong enough to be incomplete. They know they are human beings, not gods. They know they are not perfect or without fault. They know they are not finished products. So the adult can be aware of what he knows, as well as that he coexists with the grownup internally; he is aware that what the grownup knows and believes is very different from what the adult knows as reality. It is possible to be aware of your ignorance and knowledge at the same time. It is possible to know that you have powers but feel powerless in some ways just the same. This is the "both/and" adult perspective.

Lou had a young client named Jason who, in a short time, had built up a million-dollar business from scratch. Jason came to Lou mystified about why he couldn't seem to keep other young executives in the company. New technologies and ideas were passing him by, and he couldn't stand the threat of failure he lived with constantly. As the company grew, Jason hired capable managers—one in particular who was talented and affable and often took on extra work eagerly. However, if the work wasn't done exactly as Jason would have done it, he was dissatisfied and critical and let it be known that the job was only half right. In public, he was abusive in his criticisms and had more than once told his employee, "If you want a promotion—" and then he'd interject a derogatory name, "you'd better learn to do things right." Jason carried a list in his pocket of all the deals they had missed, and often read it aloud as a way to keep his staff on their toes.

The managers were so intimidated by Jason that they told him only what they knew he wanted to hear. His company was beginning to show the effects of a faulty feedback system, but no one would tell him the difficulties they were having. Especially in situations where teamwork was necessary, they were losing accounts. People would not offer their points of view for fear of being ignored, put down, or—worse—used as an example of "what's wrong with this company."

Jason was a very skilled and bright grownup who thought that all you had to do was bully people the way he had bullied himself to get his company off to such a great start. Had a conscious adult been wielding his considerable powers, Jason would have known that the company was not a one-person operation: that everyone on the team had to be listened to, and know they are heard, if the decision-making process is to be fully informed.

Adults know that the ability to listen is a power. Jason had the power to listen to his own needs, and to industry voices, but he lacked the power to listen to his team. He was unaware of his deficiency. He just assumed that his early success meant that he had the golden touch when it came to business. The limits were someone else's fault.

After many stressful encounters with Jason, the managers presented him with a unified front, detailing what was not working for the company. Jason failed to hear them. Several of the best managers left, among them the particularly talented colleague he had such great hopes for. Another company's executive, on hearing of Jason's loss, asked him incredulously, "How could you let a guy like that go?" Jason's former employee was snapped up by the competition within hours.

Despite Jason's business smarts, he had a grave lack of interpersonal skills. His need to remain unconscious about his limitations translated into the company's growing loss of control in the marketplace. Jason used his skills to dominate, disparage, control, and demand perfection, rather than to provide informed and focused leadership for his company team. In feeding the grownup's survival needs, Jason lost the power to listen, to communicate based on what he heard, and to negotiate in a way that would allow him to benefit from his talented employees and their ideas. In fact, just the opposite occurred, and the competition benefited.

In Jason's experience, we can see the differences between adult functioning and grownup functioning around the issue of limits. Adults make conscious, deliberate use of personal power, whereas grownups like Jason make unconscious use of their personal power. The adult is aware of areas in which he is powerful—in being able to think well and clearly, for example—and can take pleasure in exercising that power. The grownup, on the other hand, is denied such ownership and satisfaction. Because of success in one area, Jason assumed that a broad base of powers were at his disposal (in this case, dominance and control). His success fed his fantasy of achieving perfection, which kept his limits safely out of his own line of vision. He had no conscious knowledge about where and in what situations his power was real, and where and in what ways he was limited.

Adults can seek and use feedback, including negative feedback that makes them uncomfortable. One good friend of ours, who regularly seeks feedback from her teammates and employees, says that she hates the feelings negative feedback produces in her, but she knows that if she doesn't listen and learn, she can't create the changes necessary to stay successful in her business and her relationships.

Grownups confronted with their limitations operate in the emergency prevention response mode. Their internal attention is usually much more focused on avoiding the dreaded catastrophe of exposure than on a conscious awareness of their options, limits, personal powers, and abilities. All the grownup knows is that she must respond to a limit, and she often does so effectively, although without the experience of a fully considered choice.

Adults by definition have internal *permission* to increase their personal power, whereas grownups have an internal, psychological *demand* to increase or limit theirs. Adults also have permission to experience the pleasure and delight of exercising and improving their personal power, whereas grownups take no pleasure from the exercise of personal power in itself, but often delight in the downfall of others. Because grownups unconsciously experience themselves as flawed, they can get a temporary boost from sensing that someone else is in even worse shape. Psychologists (and Germans) call this *Schadenfreude*—pleasure in someone else's misfortune.

Living with Your Limits

Grownups are unconsciously forbidden to experience themselves as powerful. In fact, some grownups whose families demanded that they be powerful in a certain area—say, academics—take pleasure in proving their independence by *not* meeting that demand. But the pleasure is located more in the experience of defiance than in the experience and exercise of the power to excel (or fail, as the case may be). Adults can take pleasure from successful results and learn from their mistakes, whereas grownups live with a demand for continual successful results and the need to avoid the experience of mistakes (and, therefore, the experience of learning from mistakes).

Adults take the acceptance of their limits as a matter of course, whereas grownups experience feelings of shame around their limits: Limits for the grownup are experienced in exactly the same way as failure. Adults have a sense of clarity about the nature of the limit they're experiencing in a given moment. They are usually aware of the kind of limit they're dealing with: whether it's physical or environmental, and therefore absolute; or based on skill level, meaning that it's subject to change over time; or whether they're up against a psychologically induced limit, which is also subject to modification or even elimination. Grownups have a great deal of confusion around the nature of limits in any given moment, because being limited is, in general, so fearful and shameful that there isn't the psychological time or space to explore the nature of the limit involved.

Limits are a fact of life, whether they are inherent or self-imposed. Your relationship to your limits determines how much power they will have to affect your life. In every situation, you can choose to recognize the limits affecting you and analyze to what degree they're subject to change. Even people born with the limits of physical or mental disability must at some time in their lives choose to accept their disability in order to go on with the work of living life to the fullest.

But even when you choose to accept your limits, the effect does not automatically make life easier. A neighbor of ours, a widower, recently gave up a high-paying job in the city, because the long commute meant that he could not spend much time with his young daughter. The importance of his time with her outweighed the loss of financial security that would come with the change. He felt good about his power to choose that limitation over the limits imposed by being an absent parent. His confidence in his choice was shaken a bit when he was offered a job in the same industry at a higher rate of pay than before, but with the same drawback of a long commute. He again chose to work close to home, even though he was by now feeling the pinch of his lower salary. His comment, after reflection, was that he was glad to have the offer again so he could reexamine his priorities and reaffirm his choice to spend more time with his child, despite financial worries. In his choice of limits, he was able to experience a sense of personal power.

Adults know that they have to be clear about the powers they choose to exercise, because some powers preclude the possession of others. There is power in knowing that every choice will have a downside. When you know about this, you can include it in your plans.

You can move easily with your powers and limits when you have the steady vantage point of a strong sense of identity, separate from what you own, owe, rent, buy, join, support, challenge, or desire. A client of Lou's began to pay special attention to his dreams as part of his work of getting to know himself. He dreamed that he worked in his office, slept in his office, and played golf in his office, as well as ate and relieved himself there. He felt it was obvious that the dream was trying to tell him the extent to which he was identified with his work, but it upset him to think that without his work he would feel no sense of self.

A sense of self allows you to say: Okay, I am not my work . . . If my job (religion, political point of view, or whatever) becomes untenable, I can take my powers and limits and move on. When you don't have a separate sense of identity, you substitute the goals and values of the organization or person you have merged with for the goals and dreams that are your birthright. This is what many grownups do with their whole lives. They live the life their parents or family or company or church wants them to live.

The Fantasy of Perfection

The separate, safe, internal "I" is the bedrock of your ability to trust yourself. When you can't trust what you think or feel or experience, you are powerless to direct your own life. Over time, this trust is built not only on your successes, but on your mistakes and the self-knowledge you gain from them.

People substitute the dream of perfection for a real identity. It is a grownup dream in which you get to be all-powerful, living a life without limitation, or at least only temporarily limited until you "get it right." Part of the dream of perfection is that you can create it in your life by working hard for it. Not everyone can have it—or so the thinking goes. It is only for "special people" who are really "good"—and that's part of its seduction. In the dream of perfection, "special people" don't have to notice their limits, or else don't have any. In this dream, you can remain unconscious of your shortcomings, harmful behavior, and mistakes, because they'll be gone soon; or you don't have to be aware because you're protected by the "special covenant" you have entered.

The dream of perfection remains the driving force behind many religions, ideologies, diets, methods of education, social schemes, political campaigns, and advertisements. It is a hope, a hope that you don't have to accept yourself and your life as it is, in all its messy imperfection, but can somehow manipulate it into being perfect. It is a subtle, unspoken motivation behind much of grownup behavior, and it is maintained by a refusal to see the reality of our powers and limitations. Our powers are seen as limitless, and our limits are dismissed altogether. We can attain God, Heaven, the perfect life, the perfect partner, perfect health, the perfect body, the perfect country—if we follow the tenets of our grownup system, obey the guidelines without question, work hard, and try, try, try.

In this type of system, it is essential to see yourself as always being on the verge of perfection—because being on the verge puts you in the driver's seat. Then you can take the next step, which will be the winning step of overcoming your limits and becoming all-powerful. It is this fantasy of perfection that stands between recognizing your limits and experiencing the power that is actually available to you.

One of the most widespread strategies for actualizing the dream of perfection is to set up and idealize a person or system of thought that you *can* see as perfect. Gurus, rock stars, movie stars, and political leaders owe some of their immense power to the grownup need to count on something without question. There is nothing wrong with being vulnerable and wanting to feel safe. It becomes a liability only when it is unconscious, leading you to nurture fantasies that can never be fulfilled.

The grownup longs for certainty and security in the vain hope that they will keep change and pain at bay. Adults know that perfect security is a fantasy that cannot be achieved by childish bargaining with life or "good behavior." There is no personal power in that kind of security. Real security is based in the knowledge that change will come: It may hurt, but you have the powers to deal with it. The grownup, in contrast, tries to create a continuous experience of perfect safety and continuity without limits. Thus the grownup looks for authority figures or systems that promise that kind of perfection, the preservation of cherished ideas, or the fulfillment of the hope of being at last validated. These are grownup hopes and strategies.

That childish part of us gladly gives up independence and power to conform to anything that promises protection from the consequences of our limitations. The grownup wants to know that everything will turn out right—which is a euphemism for *his way*—that he never has to worry again, and that he'll get everything he wants if he just behaves. The success of cults is directly related to the amount of safety they promise in this world and the next. What the grownup doesn't know is that powers exist inside himself which, if he develops them, will give him the satisfaction and serenity he seeks. The adult knows this and rests in that knowledge right alongside the grownup fantasies of perfection that everyone—no matter how self-aware—entertains.

The search for security, as opposed to the development of adult power, is a grownup obsession. This search for security translates into rigidity of behavior. A man we interviewed told us of his experience of that quality in his own life. He was a "hero" type in his family and exercised considerable powers in that role. He was compelled to shine in every way to make his family look good, so he developed many of his powers and received many rewards. To this day, our "hero" confesses that he can't stop being loyal, authoritative, and helpful, a "rock to depend on," even continuing to give financial support to a minister he knows to be guilty of stealing church funds. This grownup hero has not yet developed the standpoint of a separate identity outside of the role he was assigned to play in his family of origin.

Another form of security-seeking that prevents the perception of limits involves acting as if you will live forever. We all know people, especially teenagers, who don't seem to know that their time on earth is limited. When you become willing to wake up both to your mortality and your limits, you are at an important turning point in your life. When you let in the knowledge of your true condition as a mutable, imperfect human being, you are suddenly in a position to make reality-based choices about how to relate to yourself and others.

It is hard to let that knowledge in and not lose your focus. Your internal "I" needs to be strong and centered in the knowledge of your humanity and in your ability to learn, to become open to an awareness of how limited you are. Denying the presence of limits in our lives is a waste of time and energy. Doing so blocks the experience of creativity in dealing with those limits. We are robbed of the full experience of our lives. A friend of ours told us how her relationship with her daughter has been expanded and enriched. "It took being confronted by my daughter about how I had messed up as a parent. Even though it was really hard for me, I was finally able to hear what she was saying. I kept reminding myself that I'm not perfect, and she's not either. The honest intimacy we now have between us was worth every bit of the work it took to get our relationship straightened out."

When your need for safety is unconscious, you look for security and perfection. When you can admit your limitations, you can then be open to the use of your creativity to solve your problems, restoring and repairing the damage you have suffered and inflicted. Repair and restoration are an antidote to the need for perfection.

Letting the Grownup and the Adult Live Side-by-Side Within You

One of your powers is knowing that you have limits—and recognizing and respecting them. We are all psychologically wounded, even if we didn't grow up in abusive families. It hurts to know that you and those you love will suffer and die and that you are powerless to prevent it. It hurts at first to realize that you don't know everything and will *never* know all the answers. Change is painful, too, and—perhaps ironically—is a constant fact of life. Adults can accept this knowledge of their limits. They know that limits are part of being human. Grownups are compelled to keep this knowledge out of consciousness.

This difference in the relationship to power on the part of the grownup and the adult also has a bearing on the internal relationship between the adult and the grownup within each of us. The grownup self can create very strong, internal psychological states—so strong, in fact, that they can interfere with the adult's capacity to exercise certain powers. Chronic depression, rages, and other emotional overloads, passivity, and constant emergency thoughts and feelings come from wounds lodged in grownups' psyches.

When your internal world is captured by these states, it's easy to lose contact with your adult self. Adults, although not liking it, realize that in a given moment the balance of power within may be shifted in favor of the defensive needs of the wounded grownup. The adult can respond to reality as it is and make choices about what's possible, what's impossible, and which power to call on. This includes responding to the internal impact of the grownup self's defensive reactions.

Let's take a water phobia again as an example. Such a phobia is invariably a symptom of an unhealed wound of the grownup. The adult can be aware that a part of himself is terrified of the water and can have the experience of approaching the water and being so overcome with terror that his body is literally unable to proceed. The adult accepts that as his reality for the moment and can use his intellect and creativity to choose to develop a strategy for working to overcome the phobia. The adult is not ashamed of, and does not need to hide from, this inner limit. On the other hand, ignoring the fearful state and throwing himself in the water might be the solution his grownup side would choose; or perhaps he would choose to ignore the whole thing completely, claiming that he doesn't like the water anyway.

The adult knows that these strategies would only create more resistance and less accessibility to the part of himself containing the roots of the dysfunction. The adult self is allowed to seek help in finding techniques for working with the phobia that do not require denying or minimizing its reality. Adults can learn these techniques and choose to apply them. Our adult self must be willing to accept our internal grownup self on its own terms, to be compassionate and understanding about the unhealed wound the grownup carries and is trying to manage, and to do what heals and helps.

The adult self grows by expanding contact with the grownup self, not by trying to deny it or wipe it out. We cannot say this strongly enough: The adult part of us grows in compassion and wisdom by paying attention and being loving to the wounded part of us. (See Bradshaw's *Homecoming: Reclaiming and Champi-*

oning Your Inner Child and Kabat-Zinn's *Full Catastrophe Living: Using the Wisdom of Your Body to Face Stress, Pain, and Illness* for excellent suggestions on healing inner wounds.) As Ken Wilber wrote in an article for *Common Boundary:* "Until you work out unresolved issues lodged in the unconscious, they stand in the way of higher development."

The grownup has a more complicated internal relationship to the power of the adult. At some level, your grownup self needs and wishes for the awareness and understanding of your adult self. However, as a result of past abandonment, there is an automatic and deeply programmed response of fear and suspicion around any adult, including your own internal adult self. As a friend put it, "My grownup self is very, very defensive of her turf. It's as if she is the older child who has taken care of an entire household for years and then, suddenly, a stepmother comes onto the scene."

The grownup self is caught in a double bind in that she needs the internal adult to be powerful and to take care of the unhealed wounds that limit her, but at the same time she is fearful of that exercise of power and the exposure of her wound. She will be frightened by the adult's freedom to act in the outside world in general, and in relationships in particular, in ways that she has been taught to think of as weak or dangerous—for example, asking for help, acknowledging ignorance, or seeking emotional intimacy. So the grownup paradoxically will often seek to undermine her own adult power.

Chuck Jones, the famous animator of Wile E. Coyote and Bugs Bunny, is quoted in *The Creative Spirit* (Goleman et al.) as saying: "I've never made a picture in my life drawing animated cartoons in which I didn't face this monster, fear . . . Anxiety is the handmaiden of creativity. But it's the recognition and the willingness to engage it that matters." Although there are inherent fears in letting go and facing the unknown, we believe that the grownup's fear of his own internal world is the first fear that many of us have to face in order to reclaim and expand our genuine power, creative or otherwise. The incredible limit set by the learned fear, and avoidance of our own inner unknown, must be challenged in order to become conscious, fully empowered adults.

When you deal with your limitations, you receive special gifts from them. Even though it's hard to let in your vulnerability and the incompleteness of your knowledge, good things come from doing so. You gain access to spirituality and community. Unless you can continually make contact with your limits, you will have no awareness of your need or desire for spirituality or community. If, in your grownup mode, you believe that there is nothing as powerful or invulnerable as yourself, and nothing you don't know, there is no sense of anything above and beyond you that is a mystery. You then have no reason to form the relationship to the unknown that we call spirituality (see the Ulanovs' book, *Primary Speech: A Psychology of Prayer*), or to seek out your fellow human beings so that you can help each other and make life easier for all. In their book *The Spirituality of Imperfection,* Kurtz and Ketcham make the point that "spirituality helps us first to see, and then to understand, and eventually to accept the imperfection that lies at the very core of our human be-ing. Spirituality accepts that 'If a thing is worth doing, it is worth doing badly.'"

When we can give up the fantasy of perfection and can stop blaming God for the trials we imagine He personally earmarked for us, we can accept our limits—however they came to us—for the everyday realities they are in our life, and get on with creative solutions or creative resignation. To quote again from the

Spirituality of Imperfection, "For literally thousands of years, sages and saints have explored the ordinary and everyday in the attempt to understand the extraordinary and divine. The ritual of the Japanese tea ceremony—simply carrying and serving tea—is a profound spiritual exercise. The posture of kneeling in prayer conveys acceptance and mindfulness. Standing up in a crowded room and saying, 'My name is John, and I'm an alcoholic' calls forth the spiritual realities of humility, gratitude, tolerance, and forgiveness . . . To be human is to embody a paradox, for according to that ancient vision, we are less than gods, more than beasts, yet somehow also both."

Your own life as it is is worth living. The spiritual leader, Rabbi Zusya, is quoted by Kurtz and Ketcham in *The Spirituality of Imperfection:* "In the coming world, they will not ask me: 'Why were you not Moses?' They will ask me: 'Why were you not Zusya?'" Each of us needs to claim the validity of our own life as it is—not for anyone else, but for ourselves.

As Kurtz and Ketcham write, "The spirituality of imperfection speaks to those who seek meaning in the absurd, peace within the chaos, light within the darkness, joy within the suffering—without denying the reality and even the necessity of absurdity, chaos, darkness, and suffering. . . . The spirituality of imperfection begins with the recognition that trying to be perfect is the most tragic human mistake."

Grownups are forced into seeking perfection (or despair, its corollary) by their need to remain unconscious of the overload of shame they carry within them. Adults can tolerate the conscious experience of this shame and can thereby initiate healing spiritual experience. Limits, in a conscious life, are also doorways and windows.

Releasing Unnatural Limits

Here's an exercise you can use to release a learned, unnatural limit. Imagine, as in the exercise in chapter 8, that you've been invited to join a play as one of the actors. Only now the character you've been assigned to play is yourself minus some limit you've learned to think of as yours. For example, you are yourself without your sense of feeling clumsy. Or you are yourself and you don't have any problem with numbers. Or you are yourself and you have no trouble at all expressing your feelings. Create a picture in your mind's eye of yourself as this character who is both less and more than you are now. Hear your voice. Feel your body. Get as clear a sense as you can of how you as this character without the limit would behave and feel and move in the world. Now imagine that you are playing this character in a real-life situation in which being free of whatever limit you've chosen would be useful or wonderful. Imagine this fully. Then write down how it felt to be this character and what was different about the way you behaved: How did you move, think, and speak differently than you normally do? How did it feel to move, think, and speak this way? Notice that you created this experience. What did you learn?

CHAPTER TEN

CHAPTER TEN

Reflections on a Society of Authentic Adults

*"The earth is our mother. Whatever befalls her befalls the sons
and daughters of the earth. This we know. All things are connected...
We did not weave the web of life, we are merely a strand in it. Whatever
we do to the web we do to ourselves."*

—Squamish Chief Seattle

A society that was made up of a majority of adults as we have
described them would be quite different from the world we live
in now. Any illusion that the society was perfect, or needed to
be, would only have the briefest duration. There would be a general awareness that we all have a shadow side that remains largely
hidden from us. The arrogance of people who believe that they
know all there is to know—even about themselves—would be clear
to see.

There will always be people who have no interest in being
adults or in acting responsibly toward one another. But the majority of people would see grownup behavior in themselves and
others for what it was and wouldn't glorify or abet it by responding out of an emergency prevention mode. Rather, they would
have the self-confidence to take whatever time they needed to
respond with consciousness and an open mind in most situations. This majority would be able to accept the inherent difficulties and limitations presented by life, and they would likewise
be open-minded enough to accept the presence of both the good

and the bad in the world. They would work to bring ease where difficulties exist, to solve the problems that are solvable, and to accept their own limits and those of others with grace, serenity, and a sense of humor. Most of all, they would be able to love themselves and others, and celebrate the abundance and beauty of life. They would savor each moment; they would know how to relax and how to let go.

When feedback in such a world triggered fear, shame, or defensiveness, people would recognize the source of their emergency prevention response and would be able to claim their reactions as their own. They would also feel safe enough to explore their reactions with creativity and compassion.

Husbands and wives, parents and children, teachers and students, bosses and employees, diplomats from different countries, heads of state, religious teachers and their disciples—all would exist in more respectful relationships with each other based on mutual respect. The understanding and acceptance of the reality that no one person or group has it all figured out would be prevalent, as well as acceptance of the fact that we are truly all in this together—that our collective ignorance calls for our collective intelligence. Insults that would once have led to combat would be more of a rarity. Tension would be greatly reduced, because most people would understand the difference between actual emergencies and emergency feelings resulting from unhealed wounds.

Spontaneity and playfulness would become more and more a part of adult life, because the risk of being judged or criticized would no longer be considered such a threat. The feeling of shame would not necessarily be a thing of the past, but it would no longer be something to flee. People could speak of their shame and seek solace for it, as well as look for the information contained within it. Hatred, dismissal, denial, and the need to destroy or diminish would all be seen as signs to look more deeply within before reacting out of these emotions.

Conscious adults would come from all levels of society. Becoming an adult is not the special task of any one group, but poverty and ignorance make the process much more difficult to achieve. Perhaps in this ideal world, poverty and ignorance would have given way to creative problem-solving motivated by the understanding that what happens to one member of our community affects all of us, whether we are aware of it or not.

Global Consciousness

With the rise of telecommunications and computer technology, the world is indeed getting smaller by the minute. It is abundantly clear that we are all in this together. The laws of ecology apply on a human as well as an environmental scale: One group's misery is a deficit for the entire planet. One child's hunger means that all children, in the long run, will suffer in ways we cannot even tell. We fill our jails without much thought about what sorts of citizens are being formed there—how a culture of brutality cannot be contained by any walls. We abandon whole populations of children, forgetting that these children will someday grow up into thwarted men and women filled with righteous anger and a desire for revenge.

We can no longer afford the brand of isolated individualism that is so celebrated in this country. Neither can we afford communities of unconscious citizens who believe that the reality they are most familiar with is the only one, or even the only good one; or that the problem is either somebody else or somebody else's to deal with. What we need, and hopefully are evolving toward rapidly enough, is a critical mass of conscious adults who know that they are imperfect, flawed, and capable of hurtful behavior, but are passionately interested in learning about themselves and their impact on others and their environment in general.

We live in a world where our planetary survival and progress depend more and more on groups of people working effectively together. This has become painfully clear in both the world of business and the world at large. In both these arenas, the United States has suffered a sense of many losses in the past decade or two. We lost our edge in the business of doing business, and we have lost our sense of community. In the business world, the United States had to awaken to the reality that it no longer dominated world competition. In the realm of our social communities, old and new intolerances have intensified, and the sense of isolation, division, and lack of common direction grows steadily among us.

For most of us born in the first half of this century, the rules of doing business and the structures of community were givens, already defined. Those rules and structures have been radically altered. We have been stripped of many of the outside realities that defined us.

People of this era are somewhat like a man who has been single all his life, used to living alone and fairly set in his ways, who marries a woman with four children from a previous marriage. His context changes completely and swiftly. He can no longer define himself as a solo operation. Let's say that the children range in age from two to fourteen. Simple things—like who puts what where, using the bathroom, deciding on what to eat, what to do, what to spend money and energy on—all become matters of negotiation among competing needs and radically different perspectives. This man is now a member of a community that he did not entirely choose nor create. He fell in love with his wife; her children were part of the merger. He is going to have to develop a relationship with each of those children if the marriage is going to work. And he is not the father, but the stepfather, who has all or most of the responsibilities of a father, without the benefit of certain givens that a father has. The early period of indiscriminate and unconditional bonding that children experience with their parents has already passed by the time our man arrives on the scene. This early bonding gives a parent a seemingly infinite amount of unearned power and credibility with a child. A parent who has been around through this period of development can do an awful lot wrong, and be very hurtful to a child, but the child will still look up to him and need him. The parent also has established that sense of unconditional love upon which he will draw repeatedly throughout the child's life for patience and compassion when dealing with the child. A stepparent has none of these advantages. To make things worse, he will have to develop relationships with children who have already suffered the loss of their father and are going to have some extra reluctance to become close to a surrogate dad.

Our communities, our businesses, our world have become like stepfamilies. We are simultaneously stepparents and stepchildren within these newly merged families. We loved life, and life moved in with stepchildren and stepparents in tow; and now we've got to figure out how to make it work for everybody. As a stepparent or a stepchild, I cannot take for granted my relationship with you. I am going to need to find out about you, what your needs are, what motivates you, what your shadow side harbors; and likewise you will have to find out about me.

We will first have to come to some agreement—and pretty quickly—about the practical stuff of living and working together.

Then we'll have to get to the harder stuff of what kind of family we want to be and how we make this happen. It is the same in our business worlds and our communities. If we don't talk to one another honestly, and plan practically, we will be in serious trouble.

The old givens about power and authority and family bonds are not there in the same way they used to be. It's irrelevant to debate whether they should be or not. They are not and cannot be. New and creative social contracts need to be forged. The individual, social, and political freedom to evolve has pushed us to a point where taking anything for granted is self-destructive. The lag time between taking something for granted and the pain of consequences is becoming shorter and shorter. Environmental, social, and political choices made decades ago—choices that ignored the reality that we are all in this together—are catching up with us rapidly. Our hazardous waste; our broken inner cities; and our racial, gender, ethnic, age, class, political, religious, and geographic prejudices have all born fruit now—and it's bitter, poisonous fruit. The United States has from its inception announced a desire to achieve freedom and equality for all. And yet our history can be recounted in terms of the many barriers to achieving those ideals we've encountered and created along the way. We should not look at the times when we've stumbled as evidence of our failure, but rather as part of the process of attaining our goals. An honest confrontation with all the internal and external stumbling blocks we're up against would be a sign of our commitment to the values of the founding fathers, as well as a sign of moving more fully into adulthood as a nation.

Conscious adults grasp and accept that the givens have changed. They know they will make mistakes in their lives and that they are powerless to avoid mistakes that will cause damage to themselves and those they love. They recognize the enormous gaps in their knowledge and they are already formulating their questions. But they do not feel as though they have to know all the answers in advance. They are confident in their ability to learn. They know that mistakes are not emergencies, but rather are precious sources of information. They know they can repair some damage, and also that damage is sometimes irreparable. They have given up the fantasy of perfection, because they know how destructive it is. They accept themselves and others as flawed but lovable nonetheless.

Adults can listen in an intelligent and creative way that allows them to make good use of the information they gather. They know that no matter how uncomfortable it may be, all they have is this moment, and that everything they need is contained within it. They are not afraid of their "stepchildren" or "stepparents" and have no need to dominate, or diminish, or deny them. They know that each person is totally separate from every other and that we cannot change or compromise each other's basic reality, validity, or value. They know that we are going to have to learn to communicate and work together. These are the new givens.

Because they are not ashamed of the feeling of shame, conscious adults can afford to look foolish. This allows them to be spontaneous, not take themselves too seriously, be able to play with a situation and the other players in it, move with the swirl of responses from inside and outside, stay in close contact with their own personal power, and maintain an openness to experiencing some glimpse of the unknown. If they reach an impasse, they spontaneously look for help. If they get lost and frozen in some reaction based in past wounds, it won't be long before this is recognized and they begin to talk about it. Adults do not have to remain alone in the personal hells that lead to despair and suicide. They are able to ask for help, because they know that they are worth helping. They see too much value in their lives and in life in general for suicide to ever present itself as the best option.

Adults know that sharing pain deepens intimacy. They accept that they are sometimes powerless to choose or control their own inner state and they know how devastating this can feel. They also know that this is par for the course. At those times when they feel stuck, they can call on the perspective and compassion of others.

Accepting Reality

The fact of the matter is that none of this is new. Rather, the reality is just breaking through our collective unconscious. The number of people in the world, and the increasing speed of our communications, have forced us into seeing that we are indeed a stepfamily, and have always been. When we were living so far apart—in a world that was less efficiently laced together by travel and telephones and computers—it was easier to pretend that something happening in one part of the world didn't affect things elsewhere. Now we know better.

Conscious adults know that their community is a stepfamily, as is the group of people each of us works with, as is the world at large. Their inner sense of self is not threatened by this increase in the number of "strangers" in their family. The adult's younger, wounded self may feel threatened by these strangers, and an emergency prevention response may be triggered. But the adult has the perspective to understand that this is no fault of the strangers', but rather the consequence of deficits from childhood. Adults know in their dealings with strangers that they will encounter many who are even more emotionally malnourished or wounded than they are and that this must be kept in mind as they try to relate to and work with each other. The adult recognizes that we are all a mixed bag of adult and grownup, with the balance between the two shifting and changing continuously.

The adult tries to distinguish between the areas in which another person can respond as an adult and those in which a person may be locked in to grownup behavior and automatic responses. Adults know when they are in contact with a malnourished self locked inside a grownup; they know this intuitively. They can sense a lack of open contact, and a facade that speaks of guardedness. The facade may be very smooth and shiny and charming and well intentioned, or it may be murderous. But its essential quality of guardedness is plain to the adult, who can make choices accordingly about how to interact, how much to give, and how much to hold back. The adult is capable of a "wait-and-watch" mode.

In families, communities, and the workplace, the conscious adult is able to see and be with reality as it is. The grownup self needs to manipulate reality, and the conscious adult can accept and work with the grownup's need. Ultimately, though, adults know that reality is what it is, and they start from there. This isn't a matter of resignation, but rather a sense of contact with the dynamic present—moving into and through it instead of away from it, finding out more about it, experimenting with responses, learning from feedback, looking for help, giving help where they can, and stopping to rest if the contact becomes overwhelming. This dynamic present includes the adult's own *inner* state as well as outside reality. When the inner state needs attending to, adults are ready to respond with compassion and an open mind.

After reading an early draft of this book, one of our colleagues shared an experience he'd had with his daughter when she was a teenager. "I had gotten the idea," he told us, "a 'good' idea, that Emily needed a particular kind of help in order to get on with her life at a time when she was feeling very stuck and disempowered. I was pushing her to get the help, and felt in the process like I was being a caring and responsible parent by doing so. It had gotten down to her making one last phone call. When I got home, and she told me she had not made the call, I said to her in an angry tone, 'You didn't?' My conscious adult barely caught my tone of voice. The next thing I knew, Emily was crying and saying, 'I feel like you're never satisfied with me.' It was very unlike her to cry, and she had never said this to me before. Thank God, my adult self really heard her, and I was stopped in my tracks. Far from being helpful—which had been my fantasy about the situation—I realized there was something I was doing that was giving her the message that she wasn't good enough. I was truly shocked and puzzled, because I had been conscious *only* of being helpful. But my adult could let in the feedback that perhaps more was going on than I was conscious of and that I needed help from my daughter in order to find out what it was. As it turned out, I needed help from other family members as well. Because my conscious adult was present enough, I was able to let go of being right, and simply say, 'Let's get Mom and your sister and talk about this. The last thing in the world I want you to feel is that I'm never satisfied with you.'

"We all sat down and, after everybody had their say, the consensus was that I needed to back off and let my daughter decide for herself what she needed to do to feel like she was moving forward in her life. Not that we should not all talk about it, but that I should stop interfering and manipulating her into doing what I thought was good for her. The conversation led further to the realization that she knew what it was she loved and wanted to do in her life, which was music, but had never felt that this career path was open to her. It was as if the more we talked, the more all of our conscious adults entered the conversation. There was sadness and relief, confusion and discovery, but there was no emergency. There was a problem, and we were going about solving it. Our collective creativity started to bubble, and we moved from the hopelessness contained in our unhealed wounds to the budding excitement of possibility that contact with our personal power elicits. It was in that conversation that our daughter began seriously moving toward becoming the accomplished musician she is today. It's a particularly difficult career path, but it's *her* path, and she is connecting with her power by following it."

The power to look within and get to know our deeper and often unconscious motivations is lost if we do not acknowledge our inner lives. Our colleague had lost it with his daughter, in being so driven by his unconscious need for her success and in assuming that all his motives were both conscious and good. Looking within is a tool an adult uses. It demands that we take time to look carefully at what surrounds an event, result, situation, or quality; who is involved and how; and what the effects are for everyone involved, including the grownup selves hidden in the shadows. With this perspective, the conclusions we come to will tend to be more open-minded, compassionate, and unique to the situation. Most of us are uneven in our ability to reflect within, being better at it in some areas of our lives and less skilled in others. This ability to reflect is further hampered if the stresses and strains of poverty and ignorance have the upper hand, and we are struggling just to survive.

And yet this flexibility, openness to learning, connection to

—
233

the world's shifting and complex realities, and autonomy of the adult self are what keep us connected to the truth of Chief Seattle's words quoted at the beginning of this chapter. That paradox of being totally part of, and yet totally separate from, is the adult experience of being in reality. Being able to hold this paradox in your mind allows an effectiveness and richness of experience that would not be possible to someone operating out of grownup principles. In so many ways, grownups are exiled from their own lives.

The Operating Principles of Adulthood at Work

Individuals in whom the adult is in charge have arrived at an awareness that they alone decide what is included or not included in their identity—their "me." Adults are their own source of identity. Paradoxically, their inner sense of separateness and safety opens them to feedback from, and deep connection with, the surrounding world of people and processes. Feedback can be welcomed and sought out as part of the process of self-discovery and learning. Being fundamentally self-defining and self-validating, adults do not have to worry about losing their identity or value. In the adult state, you know that if feedback does seem threatening, your grownup defenses and beliefs have kicked in. You simply need to reflect on what fear has been touched in you, be with that, and then move on.

A number of years ago, Lou served as a consultant to a group of six high-level, high-powered executives who were part of a very successful organization. He had contracted with them to help improve the fullness of their feedback to each other as a way of tapping more powerfully into their collective intelligence and inventiveness. They knew they needed this boost if they were to deal successfully with the changes in their company and the marketplace. By the time Lou had worked with the group for several months, they had made several key agreements among themselves and instituted a weekly meeting to facilitate communication with their adult selves fully present.

Their training with Lou focused on listening and the experience of being heard. One way of knowing whether the conscious adult or the grownup is in charge within a person is to observe how he or she listens and responds in a dialogue or group discussion. Conscious adults can do two things at the same time that the grownup cannot: hold an opinion of their own, and fully entertain someone else's—really see an issue from another person's point of view. If, by analogy, the discussion was going on through the medium of clay instead of words, the conscious adult could make a very clear and detailed clay model depicting his or her vision of the situation, and could also be very interested in watching colleagues make their own models depicting their own vision or point of view. The models may be completely different or they may have similarities—but they are unlikely to ever be exactly the same. The adult is interested in discovering information through the exchange, not in establishing dominance.

It is hard for all of us to have a strong opinion about something and at the same time listen to someone else's opinion—especially if it differs from our own. This group of executives had acknowledged this difficulty, agreed among themselves that it was not a crime, and decided that there was a tremendous value in improving their listening and communication skills. The restrictions placed on us by grownup operating principles need to be acknowledged up front before the conscious adult can be free to reign in these high-powered, high-stakes situations. It was made clear to everyone from the start that they were all expected as individuals who had worked their way to the top to have a strong ego that might sometimes get in the way of teamwork, to get defensive at times—in other words, to be thrown into an emergency prevention response, to have a powerful need to be "right," and a tendency to dominate and control others, be judgmental, have hidden agendas, competitiveness, embarrassment about mistakes, and an urgent need to avoid feeling shame.

It took time for the members of this group to be able to admit much of this information into their conscious awareness. Lou told them at the beginning that everyone—not just high-powered executives—carries around a full array of grownup baggage, and that one of the most devastating lessons we are taught as children and grownups is that it is possible to be completely free of this baggage (and that you *should* be free of it). The conscious adult has been disabused of this notion, recognizing it as an illusion that hopelessly gums up communication and learning. Another name for the illusion is perfectionism.

We have never known anyone sane who has said and believed, "I am perfect" or "I know I can become perfect if I work hard enough at it." Everybody, on an intellectual level, will say "Hey, I'm not perfect." But we have also never known anybody who does not have some difficulty with criticism, as well as difficulty admitting to their faults, errors, and flaws. It is this difficulty of admission that is the real problem. If it were truly all right to say, "I'm having some difficulty hearing what you are saying, because my defenses are up," the need to cover anything up would be diminished, and the learning process could progress.

To open up the atmosphere in the meeting with the executives, several preliminary actions had been taken. One of these was for group members to give and receive feedback on how each of them had contributed to, and interfered with, the use of the group meeting thus far. Each member was asked to first give an assessment of him/herself in this regard and then to evaluate the others. This amounted to an inventory of what had worked and what had not worked up until the present moment. Given their blanket permission to own their grownup as well as their adult reactions, the executives were able to go through this exercise with their focus on learning about the facts as well as the distortions, and not on scoring points.

The group came to feel reconnected to their strengths and clearer and more accepting of their blocks. Out of these preliminary discussions, they established safe signals with each other when one or more of them was communicating in some way that was impeding the group's progress (for instance, the "time-out" signal, or the use of the phrase, "You're doing your thing"). They got better and better at dealing with such problems in the moment.

The group members also decided to institute a guideline that says *Listen until heard, and speak until listened to*. They wanted to establish that it was everybody's responsibility—both speaker and listener—to make sure that communication always took place on a meaningful level. This group comprised people with a great collective sense of humor. There was more often than not a period of high hilarity at the beginning of each meeting that at times spilled into the meeting proper. Sometimes this was exactly what the group needed, and sometimes not. On more than one occasion, a speaker had to interrupt the laughter by saying, "This is all very funny, but I am not being heard." Sometimes it would take a second member finally catching on before the group recognized the importance of beginning to listen again.

In one particular meeting in which it had been arranged for

Lou to be present, observe, and give feedback, the group was having a particularly difficult time getting started, and the humor was getting more and more uncomfortable. Finally one of the members said, "Look, we all know something is going on. Let's figure out what it is." As it turned out, an urgent financial issue had cropped up and needed to be discussed, but they had not been conscious of the sense that it was inappropriate for Lou to be there for that particular discussion before they all sat down. The group had learned by then to be aware of the ways in which their humor could be defensive. They were also able to accept their defensiveness and had a growing willingness to notice and talk about such behaviors. Their difficulty in getting into the substance of this particular meeting became a cue to them that something was up. The solution was simple, once the discomfort was acknowledged (adult operating principle number 3: *I am curious about everything that goes on inside me*): Lou was simply asked to leave for that part of the discussion and to come back for the rest.

The agreements this team made around the functioning of their meetings embody at least five of the seven operating principles of the conscious adult. *I am here, and you are over there* was being constantly reinforced by the agreement to *listen until heard, and speak until listened to,* as well as by the assumption of responsibility by everyone to make that happen. The acceptance of difficulty in doing this—the need to dominate, defensiveness, and so on—reflects the conscious adult's knowledge that no internal reality is too "bad" to be acknowledged, and that *I am safe and sound inside my own skin.* In dealing with difficulty right in the moment, they were acknowledging *I know there is nothing but now,* and *I always have limits,* at least for the moment. And by following these agreements and opening up the flow of the meeting, they were steadily experiencing the sixth principle: *I always have power.*

The accessibility of their intelligence and creativity had expanded in an exciting way. Their contact with their personal powers of listening and expressing keeps building to this day their sense of strength as a team. Rather than have to compete for time in the meeting and rarely experience being heard, each member now feels more and more empowered to express even the wildest ideas and can feel that these contributions are not only acknowledged, but respected as well. They have discovered many benefits to working in a group whose operating agreements are based in the principles of conscious adulthood. When a group decides to operate this way, and builds in protocols to facilitate this, there is a tremendous reinforcement and strengthening of adult awareness, power, and creativity in each of the individual members. This particular group has become a notably inspired team that is the envy of other groups inside and outside the organization.

Love and the Adult

We have seen the marvelous things that happen when couples, families, and groups of all sorts encourage the emergence of the seven operating principles of adulthood. Increased creativity, the healthy use of conflict, increased effectiveness, a deepened sense of community, strengthened autonomy, greater honesty, and a more solid connection to reality have all emerged before our eyes. In writing this book, we have tried to capture in words an evolution of the inner self that has already gained ground, to explore some of its implications, validate its reality, and encourage other people to continue this development and exploration.

For too long, the inner domain of personal awareness has been culturally locked in the territory of psychopathology or mysticism, be it esoteric or pop. You looked inside only if you were nuts or weird. If we are to move on evolutionarily, the wealth within—as well as our wounds—must be unearthed and mined for the information they hold. The awareness of a "within," and all the potential that goes with it, should be reestablished as a birthright, seen as integral to the natural process of development into adulthood.

We noticed that throughout this book we did not talk much about the relationship of these operating principles to the experience of love, or the difference between the adult and the grownup in this regard. On finishing our first and then our second draft, we wondered why. On reflection, we realized that the adult self is a being in love, whereas the grownup is a being in search of love. As we noted earlier, love is an outgrowth of intimacy. Adults live in a state of love. That is, they experience an intimate connection to themselves, and they love themselves, warts and all. That allows them to love others, warts and all. The seven principles of conscious adulthood provide an inner structure that facilitates and maximizes the flow of love to ourselves and others.

Grownups, sadly, must reject and hate pieces of themselves that have been judged at some point to be stupid, dangerous, nasty, too pretty, too smart, too aggressive, or too something or not something enough to be allowed to exist, much less be loved, fostered, or shared. This same response of rejection is applied to others, making it very hard for the grownup to give or receive love. Connecting to your grownup self is to experience the constriction of your capacity to love around the deep wounds your heart and soul have suffered. Connecting with your adult self is to experience that the nature of your being is loving and that those same wounds can be healed. A woman we know who has done a lot of work on herself told us, "I keep having this loving feeling bubble up in my heart at the most unexpected times, and I am just wondering, has this been there all along?"

Loving is about making connections. We have a zillion ways of forging connections with each other and the world around us. Being in the adult state gives you access to many more of these connections than are available to the grownup, so you can experience your life in a fuller, richer, and more satisfying way.

Bibliography

Bradshaw, John. *Homecoming: Reclaiming and Championing Your Inner Child.* New York: Bantam, 1990.

Cameron, Julia. *The Artist's Way: A Spiritual Path to Higher Creativity.* New York: Tarcher/Putnam, 1992.

Csikszentmihalyi, Mihaly. *Flow: The Psychology of Optimal Experience.* New York: Harper and Row, 1990.

———. *The Evolving Self: A Psychology for the Third Millenium.* New York: HarperCollins, 1993.

Deikman, Arthur. *The Observing Self: Mysticism And Psychotherapy.* Boston: Beacon, 1982.

———. *The Wrong Way Home: Uncovering the Patterns of Cult Behavior in American Society.* Boston: Beacon, 1990.

Erikson, Erik. *Identity and the Life Cycle.* New York: W. W. NORTON, 1980.

Estes, Clarissa Pinkola, Ph.D. *The Creative Fire: Myths and Stories About the Cycles of Creativity.* Audiotape. Boulder, CO: Sounds True Catalogue, vol. 8, no 1, Summer 1995.

Fritz, Robert. *The Path of Least Resistance: Learning to Become the Creative Force in Your Own Life.* New York: Ballantine, 1984.

Freud, Sigmund. *An Outline of Psychoanalysis.* New York: Norton, 1949.

Guggenbuhl-Craig, Adolf. *Power in the Helping Professions.* Dallas: Spring Publications, 1992.

Gendlin, Eugene T. *Focusing.* New York: Bantam, 1981.

Goleman, Daniel, Paul Kaufman, and Michael Ray. *The Creative Spirit.* New York: Dutton, 1992.

Greenberg, Jay R., and Stephen A. Mitchell. *Object Relations in Psychoanalytic Theory.* Cambridge, MA: Harvard University Press, 1983.

Hagbert, Janet. *Real Power: Stages of Personal Power in Organizations.* San Francisco: Harper, 1984

Hendrix, Harville. *Getting the Love You Want: A Guide for Couples.* New York: Harper Collins, 1988.

Jung, C. G. *Memories, Dreams, Reflections.* New York: Vintage, 1989.

Kabat-Zinn, Jon. *Wherever You Go, There You Are: Mindfulness Meditation in Everyday Life.* New York: Hyperion, 1994.

Kabat-Zinn, Jon. *Full Catastrophe Living: Using the Wisdom of Your Body to Face Stress, Pain, and Illness.* New York: Dell, 1990.

Kaufman, Gershen. *Shame: The Power of Caring.* Rochester, VT: Schenkman, 1980.

Kurtz, Ernest and Katherine Ketcham. *The Spirituality of Imperfection: Storytelling and the Journey to Wholeness.* New York: Bantam, 1992.

Lerner, Harriet Goldhor, Ph.D. *The Dance of Intimacy: A Woman's Guide to Courageous Acts of Change in Key Relationships.* New York: Harper and Row, 1989.

Maslow, A. H. *The Farther Reaches of Human Nature.* New York: Compass, 1971.

Merser, Cheryl. *Grownups: A Generation in Search of Adulthood.* New York: Penguin, 1990.

Miller, Alice. *The Untouched Key: Tracing Childhood Trauma in Creativity and Destructiveness.* New York: Doubleday, 1990.

Paul, Margaret, Ph.D. *Inner Bonding: Becoming a Loving Adult to Your Inner Child.* New York: HarperCollins, 1992.

Peck, M. Scott. *The Road Less Traveled: A New Psychology of Love, Traditional Values, and Spiritual Growth.* New York: Simon and Schuster, 1978.

Perls, Frederick S., M.D., Ph.D. *Gestalt Therapy Verbatim.* Moab, UT: Real People Press, 1969.

Peters, Tom. *The Tom Peters Seminar: Crazy Times Call for Crazy Organizations.* New York: Vintage, 1994.

——. *Liberation Management: Necessary Diorganization for the Nano-second Nineties.* New York: Ballantine, 1992.

Ray, Michael, and Rochelle Myers. *Creativity in Business.* New York: Doubleday, 1989.

Saint Exupéry, Antoine de. *The Little Prince.* New York: Scholastic, 1943.

Seinfeld, Jeffrey. *The Empty Core: An Object Relations Approach to Psychotherapy of the Schizoid Personality.* Northvale, NJ: Jason Aronson, 1991.

Senge, Peter. *The Fifth Discipline: The Art and Practice of the Learning Organization.* New York: Doubleday, 1990.

Trungpa, Chogyam. *Cutting Through Spiritual Materialism.* Berkeley, CA: Shambala, 1973.

Ulanov, Ann and Barry Ulanov. *Primary Speech: A Psychology of Prayer.* Atlanta: John Knox, 1982.

Wilber, Ken. *The Spectrum of Consciousness.* Wheaton, IL: Theosophical Publishing House, 1977.

———. *Eye to Eye: The Quest for the New Paradigm.* Garden City, NY: Anchor, 1983.

———. "In the Full Spectrum," *Common Boundary,* May/June 1995.

Wolinsky, Stephen, Ph.D. *Trances People Live: Healing Approaches in Quantum Psychology.* Falls Village, CT: The Bramble Co., 1991.

Wood, John. *The Little Blue Book on Power.* Winslow, WA: Zen 'n' Ink.

Conari Press, established in 1987, publishes books on topics ranging from spirituality and women's history, to sexuality and personal growth. Our main goal is to publish quality books that will make a difference in people's lives—both how we feel about ourselves and how we relate to one another.

Our readers are our most important resource, and we value your input, suggestions, and ideas. We'd love to hear from you—we are publishing books for you!

For a complete catalog or to get on our mailing list, please contact us at:

CONARI PRESS

2550 Ninth Street, Suite 101
Berkeley, California 94710
800-685-9595